THE MOON IS THE KEY

The world is controlled by four super-powers—all ruled by women. Men are second class citizens.

Nuclear reactors have been banned from the earth and are controlled by an International Commission on the moon.

Roger Hanson, a member of the Commission returns to earth on leave and uncovers an audacious plot by a Male Liberation group to take over control of the world.

A football match where no holds are barred and the fans fight it out on the pitch afterwards, a Game Park where convicted criminals are turned loose and a flight in an obsolete rocket lead to an exciting and unexpected climax on the moon.

THE MOON IS THE KEY

by

Richard Lindsay

Hale SF

ROBERT HALE · LONDON

First published in Great Britain 1980

ISBN 0 7091 8420 4

Robert Hale Limited
Clerkenwell House
Clerkenwell Green
London EC1R 0HT

Photoset by
Kelly Typesetting Limited
Bradford-on-Avon, Wiltshire
and printed in Great Britain by
Clarke, Doble & Brendon
Plymouth, Devon

ONE

Hanson sat in the first-class lounge of the transit satellite and looked across the table at his Russian companion.

Mashenko was saying, "I'm looking forward so much to spending a week in England. It will be interesting to see the most advanced Matrician province in the world. We in Russia are still a long way behind."

"That's only because you started later. Our revolution had its real beginnings at the end of the twentieth century—yours began only a little more than a hundred years ago. You will soon be ahead of us."

"Now you are being too polite, I think. The truth is that we Russians are at heart a very conservative people. We do not take easily to being governed by women."

Hanson was beginning to regret the impulse that had made him suggest that Mashenko should spend a week of his leave with him in London. It had come about during one of those long, leisurely dinners which served to relieve the monotony of life in the International Moon Base. Something naïve in the Russian's earnest enthusiasm had appealed to him. And, he had to admit, years of internationalist indoctrination had not altogether cured him of some pride in his country. Now, with only a month's leave to come, he was committed to spending a quarter of it giving Mashenko a one-man guided tour.

He glanced through the observation window. The London shuttle was only a few hundred yards away in parallel orbit. There were still two others ahead of it in the queue. It would be at least an hour before they could settle down for the long flight back to London. It really was time, he thought, that another transit satellite was put into orbit round the moon. Traffic between earth and moon had almost doubled during the last two years and, now that yet another reactor had gone into operation deep below the moon's surface, the output of synthetic elements would increase sharply and strain the transport system beyond the limits of efficiency. He would make a point of discussing it when he got to London. Blanchard, the Eurasian member of the Space Transport Committee, was an old friend. He was Hanson's senior by several years, but their mothers had been at school together and they had been thrown into one another's company rather more than would normally have been the case.

Perhaps he could press for a small satellite to handle passenger traffic only and convert the present one to cargo entirely. He went over the satellite in his mind's eye, calculating the rough cost of knocking down some bulkheads, strengthening others and enlarging the docking bay.

He listened to Mashenko with only half an ear. The Russian was talking about the problems of synthesizing venusium in the new reactor. This was his particular field and he was giving a lecture rather than carrying on a conversation. Hanson was able to follow his own train of thought almost without interruption.

His leave looked like being too short. More important than either Blanchard or Mashenko was the question of his own future. At thirty-two the sands were beginning to run out for him. It was two years since he had reached the age for marriage and as yet he had done nothing about it. So far his career had gone well. Next year he would be chairman of the International Moon Commission, but after that there would be no more promotion unless he were married. Matrician society did not trust men who remained unmarried too long and excluded them from the higher echelons of the Administrative Service. Not even his mother, the Baroness Alicia Hanson, Governor of Britain and currently vice-chairman of the Eurasian Senate, could do anything about that.

There had, of course, been women in his life, but, apart from satisfying his immediate physical needs, he had got nothing from them. Men of the matrician class were forbidden to marry outside it.

When the London shuttle had docked the two men strolled into the reception area to watch the passengers disembark. There was always the chance that Hanson would meet someone he knew. But there was no-one—only a handful of Beta-class scientists and some Gamma-class technicians. After them came a dozen or so attractive-looking girls, the latest batch of moon-hostesses, specially recruited to staff the bars and the recreation centre which a thoughtful Commission had provided for the men who had to spend nine months of the year separated from their fellows by quarter of a million miles. Some of them would be lucky and find themselves husbands of a higher class; others would finish up as hostesses of quite another kind.

Neither man was interested in the girls. Mashenko, as became a dedicated scientist, scorned such frivolities. Hanson, as a senior member of the Commission, was expected to be more discreet in his liaisons. They were just about to move back into the lounge when a flurry of activity at the airlock caught their attention.

A group of men, dishevelled and unshaven, shuffled through the door. They were handcuffed together and with them were two guards, the largest women Hanson had ever seen. As well as stun-ray guns they carried heavy whips which they kept flicking about the prisoners' legs. They wore Delta-class badges on their tunics and they were ugly.

Mashenko was instantly curious. "Who are these?"

"Convicts going to the other side of the moon to dig the tunnels for your reactors. You must have seen them before."

He turned away. No doubt they deserved their punishment, but he did not care to watch other people's humiliation. Mashenko continued to stare at them. He had seen them before, space-suited figures going to their daily work in the tunnels, but this was somehow different. Suddenly he nudged Hanson. "One of these men seems to know you—he's been staring at you."

"Which one?" Hanson turned round, but the line of convicts was being chivvied through the door by the guards. He gazed after them, then shrugged his shoulders. There must be quite a number of people who recognized the Deputy Chairman of Mooncom. All the same, there had been something vaguely familiar about the back view of one of the convicts.

The whine of the shuttle's gravity reversal unit had barely died down when they stepped out into the morning sunshine. There was no wind and a faint haze hung over the Thames estuary.

A government pilot stepped forward and saluted.

"Mr Hanson, sir? Her Excellency thought you would prefer to spend your first day of leave in the country with her. The heliplane is over there. I'll collect your baggage."

Mashenko was impressed. Shuttle landing areas were out of bounds to small craft. The other passengers were climbing into the bus which would take them to the terminal building. There they would have to wait until their luggage was unloaded and sent over.

They walked slowly over to the heliplane. It was always the same, this return to earth gravity. Mashenko particularly felt it. He spent so much time in his laboratory that he had little left over for the exercise machines or the ball games in the earth-gravity gymnasium. His muscles were feeble from lack of use. Hanson, whose work was less demanding in terms of time, exercised daily, but it would be a couple of weeks before even he got used to the extra muscular effort needed for the slightest movements.

"Is it far to your mother's house?" Mashenko asked as they settled into the heliplane.

"About seventy miles—ten minutes or so. She lives there

most of the time when the Senate is not in session. She prefers it to the vice-chairman's official residence in Berlin."

The pilot climbed into his seat. The liquid hydrogen motor started up almost inaudibly and the rotor began fripping the air. Slowly the heliplane rose to two thousand feet—its regulation height—and they could see the row upon row of tall buildings that was London stretching away into the haze. The pilot cut the rotor and opened the lateral jets and the heliplane accelerated rapidly but smoothly. Twenty miles from the shuttle-port the haze cleared and they could see wide stretches of forest punctuated by clearings. Here and there were large houses surrounded by parks and areas of cultivated ground. Mashenko was intrigued. "Why so many trees?"

"Part of our policy of conservation. Ninety-eight percent of the people live in the cities. That way we use only a minimum of our natural resources."

The note of the jets changed and the rotor started up. Below them the sunlight glinted on the solar collectors of a large white house set in a park surrounded by high walls. Beyond the walls were cultivated fields and a few small houses on the edge of the forest.

The heliplane alighted gently on the lawn in front of the tall windows. As the rotor cut out a small aircar with two uniformed servants came towards them from the other side of the house.

A tall figure appeared in the doorway. At fifty-two the Baroness Alicia Hanson was still a strikingly beautiful woman. Her body was beginning to thicken slightly, but the face with its straight nose and cool grey eyes remained strangely youthful. It was almost as if it had not kept pace with the rest of her body. She did not wait to be introduced.

"I'm so glad to meet you, Mr Mashenko. I've been hearing such a lot about your work on venusium from Madame Drubetskaya."

Mme Drubetskaya was chairman of the Physical Resources Committee of the Senate. Hanson allowed the merest twitch of a grin to flit across his face. He suspected that his mother knew very little about venusium and cared less. As for Mme. Drubetskaya, she couldn't stand her at any price. She had probably been briefed by one of her secretaries ten minutes ago. It was minute attention to detail of this sort that made her such a formidable politician.

Mashenko, who had expected he knew not what . . . authority . . . arrogance . . . condescension, was instantly captivated. He bowed deeply and kissed the extended hand.

"We must have a long talk about what is happening in Russia," she continued. "I only get the official picture. You must tell me what the Russian people really feel and think."

A manservant appeared in the background.

"Briggs will show you to your rooms. You must want to have a bath and refresh yourselves before lunch."

Hanson noted that, apart from her all-embracing smile, she had more or less ignored him. That was ominous. It meant that she had one of her "serious talks" in store for him. He could guess the subject.

She had put them in adjacent rooms. When the servant had gone Mashenko came bouncing in, beaming all over his open Slav countenance.

"I had no idea your mother was such a charming woman—not at all what I had expected. I have seen her pictures, of course, but they give no idea of what she is really like—so kind and not at all overbearing. This will be something to talk about when I get back to Moscow."

"Don't let her manner deceive you—she is as hard underneath as your precious venusium. She would eat you for breakfast if she had a mind to."

"Oh no, my friend, you are too—how do you say?—cynical. You are making fun of me."

"The country air has gone to your head. Go and have a cold bath." He pushed him out of the room.

The visiphone beside the bed buzzed. He switched it on and his mother's face appeared on the screen.

"When you've had your bath, come down to the small

sitting-room. We must have a lot to talk about. I'll send one of the girls to show your friend round the gardens. I'm sure Russian gardens are different."

The image snapped off before he could reply.

When he came down she was sitting in the window looking out over the park. She motioned him to the opposite end of the window-seat.

"It's time we had a serious talk about your future." She paused as if expecting some reply. Getting none, she went on, "I understand you are to be chairman of Mooncom after your next tour." He nodded.

"And after that?"

He shrugged, "I don't know . . . there are several possibilities."

"You know I have never interfered in your life—always allowed you to go your own way."

He let that pass. "You've done well so far and now it is time you thought about getting married."

He made as if to reply, but she interrupted, "No—don't tell me you haven't found the right girl yet. Leave that sort of nonsense to people like your scientist friend. You are a matrician—you have a duty to your class and to me."

"To you?"

"Yes—to me. Your wife must take the place of the daughter I could not have. I want a granddaughter to carry on our name."

Now we are getting to it, he thought. Under English law a man normally became part of his wife's family and took her name, but exceptions were sometimes made for matrician families where there was no daughter to succeed. A woman could adopt her son's wife who would then take her name. Strictly speaking, all property belonged to the state which assigned it to women in accordance with their position and occupation. Inheritance was limited to personal chattels only. Over the last hundred years or so, however, there had gradually crept in the practice of assigning to daughters of powerful families the properties which had been occupied by their mothers. It was all perfectly legal, of course. Large estates were allocated by a committee of the Provincial Senate and membership of the Senate was limited to women of matrician families. If Hanson were to marry a younger daughter of a matrician family, he and his wife would continue to live on his mother's properties and he would not have to change his name. He knew his mother well enough to be sure that she had already lined up a selection of suitable girls . . . but not yet. He was going to make his own choice, and in his own time.

"There's no need to worry. I've been thinking about it for some time, but I don't intend to rush it. Next leave or the one after will be soon enough to make a choice. I have some projects I want to push through when I am chairman of Mooncom. They will take at least a year and I can't marry until then."

His mother nodded and said nothing. Men who got married during moon service were automatically posted to an earth appointment. She would have made the same decision herself had she been a man.

Hanson relaxed. He had won—at least for the present.

"How is my father?"

"Well enough. He is on holiday at the moment . . . in California . . . he'll be back in a few days."

Hanson always felt a little ill at ease in his mother's company. At the time of his conception she had decided that her first child had better be a boy. She was too busy making her way in the Senate to have the time to devote to bringing up a girl. Afterwards, she found that she could not have any more children and Hanson always felt that she blamed him for this, irrational as it might seem. Now he struggled to make conversation.

"What about your own career? People are saying that you are likely to be the next chairman of the Eurasian Senate."

"Yes, I hope so, but . . ." She hesitated. "There may be a problem." Hanson raised his eyebrows. It was unlike her to admit that there might be any difficulty—especially to him.

"Come into my office and I will show you something."

He followed her through to the room from which she governed the whole of Britain and did most of her Senate work as well. He had only been in it once before in his life. She did not go to her desk with its array of visiphones and computer terminals. Instead she went to a small safe concealed by a photograph of the World Praesidium of which she was a junior member. She opened it and withdrew a small sheaf of what appeared to be computer print-outs.

"Look at these."

He picked up one and scanned it. It was an analysis of factory output figures. Half-way down the sheet there was a gap in the column of figures and a sentence had been inserted.

"Men of England—how much longer are you going to be slaves to your women?"

All the other sheets had similar messages inserted in the text. One of them read, "Men of England—Malib is leading the fight for your liberation—why not join us?"

When he had finished reading them his mother said, "These messages began appearing about nine months ago—not many at first, but now there is one almost every day, each time from a different computer. No sooner is the programme corrected than a message appears in another one."

She paused and then went on, "Our security people have come up with nothing. Apart from the Credit Computer which is completely secure, all the small computer systems we use for information can be linked together, if you know the codes, and any input terminal in the country can be used to insert messages in any of them.

"About six months ago the London police were given an anonymous tip about a Malib meeting and arrested all the men there. None of them knew anything about the organization—it was their first time there. They had hoped to join it at that meeting. Since then there have been more of these anonymous tips and each time the result has been the same. None of the arrested men knew anything. They had all simply received a note at their place of work giving the time and place of the meeting."

"Has this been happening anywhere else, or is it just in England?"

"Only in this country so far as I know. I've had to be discreet, of course, but I can't keep it to myself much longer."

She did not have to spell out the implications. With a subversive organization rearing its head in the province she governed, there was small chance of her getting the chairmanship of the Senate unless she could root it out. For over a hundred years now women had ruled the world and given it peace and plenty. Starvation and poverty had been abolished and war was a thing of the past. No country had more weapons than were necessary for policing it and all the nuclear reactors in existence were buried below the surface of the moon under international control. There would always be malcontents, of course, but up till now there had not been the least whisper of revolution.

His mother went on, "If it were not for these people who have been arrested and sent to moon-labour I would have been inclined to treat it as some sort of practical joke—in fact, that is what we thought at first. With no weapons and all the potential revolutionaries walled up in the cities, I don't see how they can hope to succeed. That is what worries me most. If we knew what their objective was we could do something about it, but as it is, we know nothing, absolutely nothing."

Her tone made it clear that she was appealing for help, but Hanson judged that she was reluctant to ask outright. She had never, he imagined, asked a man for help in her life.

"I don't know what I can do if your security people have drawn a blank, but I don't mind having a try."

"I was hoping you would say that. This is a job that only a

man can do. It is a pity about your Russian friend—I suggest you take him to London for a few days and then get rid of him."

He had some difficulty in dragging Mashenko away. The Russian had never before had an opportunity to move in such exalted circles and the baroness had been at her best, listening attentively to what he had to say and flattering him with well-posed questions. She herself had contributed a dissertation on the ethos of the matrician state.

It was late afternoon when the baroness's government heliplane set them down on the roof of the block of bachelor flats at Richmond where Hanson stayed when he was in London. Strictly speaking, Richmond was not in London proper which began a mile further down the river. The metallic gleam of the city wall could be seen through the trees from the roof of the flats. On the other side of the river, again carefully screened by trees, were the huge buildings of the hydroponic farms which supplied the capital with its green vegetables. The synthetic meat factories, which gave off unpleasant odours at certain times of the day, were far away on the Essex marshes.

A lift whisked them silently down two floors and they stepped out into a wide, thickly carpeted corridor. Hanson took out his identity card and presented it to the scanner set in the door jamb. The door slid open and they went into the comfortably furnished sitting-room. Three bedrooms, each with its own bathroom, opened off it and at one end was the dining area, connected by a short passageway to the service compartment.

Mashenko was eager to go out straight away and visit the city, but Hanson said, "Don't let's rush it, there is something I want to do before we go out. I suggest you take a walk in the park to work up an appetite. Then we can have an early dinner and go out on the town."

He went to the small computer terminal concealed behind a curtain and picked up the menu book. He decided on oysters and roast wild boar followed by cheese and fresh grapes. On the moon, like anyone else, matricians had to put up with synthetic meat and frozen vegetables. Here he could eat real food and he was determined to have a good meal before they went out. He keyed the appropriate digits into the computer and a minute later confirmation flashed on the screen.

When Mashenko had gone he went to the visiphone and keyed the number of the Space Transport office. A girl wearing a Gamma-class tunic appeared on the screen and he asked for Blanchard.

"Mr Blanchard no longer works here. Mr Hughes has taken over from him, but he is out just now. Can I make an appointment for you?"

"Do you know where I can find Mr Blanchard?"

"No, I'm sorry sir, I'm new here."

This was strange. All senior appointments were gazetted as they were made but he could not recall having seen any mention of this one. He made an appointment with Hughes for ten-thirty next morning and then tried Blanchard's flat. There was no reply. Puzzled, he went to the computer terminal and asked for information from the Matrician Register. There was a few seconds' delay and the words "No Record" flashed on the screen.

There was just a possibility that the new appointment had been made in a hurry and the amended entry had not been fed in. He would leave it till the morning. Ever since his school days he had looked on Blanchard as almost an elder brother and more than once in the past he had come up with an answer to what had at the time seemed an insoluble problem. He particularly wanted to discuss the mysterious Malib messages with him.

After they had eaten they took a ground-taxi to the gatehouse built into the city wall. The uniformed guard, seeing Hanson's Matrician tunic, saluted and pushed a button on the console beside him. A narrow door slid open to reveal a passage large enough to accommodate several people. A middle-aged woman sat at a desk protected by an armour-plated screen. At the end of the passage there was a similar door controlled by a switch from the desk.

Once they were inside, the door closed behind them with a heavy click. Apart from her eyes, which were watchful and suspicious, the woman's face was devoid of expression. She asked crisply, "Cards please."

She put Hanson's card in a scanner unit and pressed a button. Seconds later, verification flashed on the screen in front of her. She looked at Mashenko's card. "This will have to be verified with Moscow. That will take some time—I'll give you a temporary pass until it comes through. You can collect your card on the way out. Mr Hanson will be responsible for you till then."

She touched a switch and the door slid open to reveal another narrow corridor. The floor was of steel and a notice on the wall informed them that it could be energized with half a million volts. The door at the other end opened on their approach and they were in a small room occupied by two female guards armed with stun-rays. The guards saluted and opened a door leading to the main concourse which served as a sort of waiting-room. There was a bar and shops selling tourist souvenirs and guides to the city.

Hanson made his way to the bar. "Let's have a drink while we decide what to do."

Mashenko, who had remained silent during their passage through the gatehouse, swallowed his drink at one gulp and asked for another. He found it all strange and not a little disquieting. They had nothing like this in Russia.

The walled city, now common throughout most of Europe and America, was a peculiarly English development. After the first Feminist Revolution at the end of the twentieth century there had been a period of confused political strife with governments changing several times a year, each more inefficient than its predecessor, until finally the country returned to the lawlessness and violence of the nineteen eighties and nineties. People had grown tired of the succession of demagogues splitting their parties into ever smaller groups whose rivalries were personal rather than political.

The second Feminist Revolution changed all that. Led by Alice Fay, the daughter of an obscure Wigan shopkeeper, who, by the time she was forty, had brought up a small family and become Professor of Political Science at Oxford, the Women's League of Order and Loyalty cleared the board in the elections of twenty thirty-two and proceeded with ruthless logic to demolish the shabby façade which was all that remained of British parliamentary democracy. Voting tests were introduced and gradually made more difficult until only a tenth of the population were entitled to vote.

Urban violence was savagely suppressed. Section by section the cities were razed to the ground and replaced by row upon row of identical living modules and larger factory modules, all covered in and connected by moving walkways. Hydroponic farms and synthetic protein factories were established on the outskirts so that each city was an independent self-contained unit and, finally, to ensure that any violence would be contained, walls were erected round them. Within a few generations of Alice Fay's death, the walled city had become the English way of life—a way of life which eventually spread across most of the western world.

All this Mashenko knew but had not directly experienced. The wars with China at the beginning of the twenty-first century had wiped out all Russia's major cities except Leningrad and millions of her people had died of starvation after the systematic defoliation of vast areas. She was still, after several generations, a mainly agricultural society. Her towns were growing slowly, but, by the standards of the rest of the world, they were spacious and thinly populated.

A large screen on one wall of the concourse displayed the entertainments available that evening. Mashenko decided that he would like to see an English football match—the oldest ball game in Europe and played better in England than anywhere else in the world.

They went to the railcar terminal. Hanson selected a two-seat car and punched out the destination digits of the football stadium. The car, balanced on its single rail, moved slowly from the parking bay to the acceleration track where it speeded up and, in seconds, slotted itself into a vacant space on the fast rail. As the car hurtled through the brightly lit tunnel Hanson explained to his guest how the control computer varied the speeds of the cars and the distance between them according to the amount of traffic circulating from one second to the next, compensating automatically for each car that joined or left the system. As they approached the stadium their speed was reduced by traffic joining the track from converging rails.

Mashenko, who had half expected to see a crowd of lifeless zombies, was surprised to see groups of men and women with strangely animated faces, wearing rosettes and carrying flags in the colours of the opposing teams. They jabbered excitedly as they hurried along to the doors of the stadium. Hanson led him into the matrician entrance and up a short staircase into a box opposite the centre of the field. On the other side of the pitch were the Beta-class seats. Both the Matrician and Beta-class seats were flanked by rows of Gammas. The rest of the stadium was occupied by Deltas and Epsilons who were not segregated. The effect of the whole was a pleasing, almost symmetrical pattern of different colours. Flags and rosettes gave colour and life to the drab greys and browns of the Deltas and Epsilons. The stadium was packed and even the matrician boxes were filled, for the match between two London teams—the Chelsea Lions and the Fulham Tigers— promised to be one of the most exciting of the year. Both teams were at the top of the league and hot contenders for the national championship.

Hanson glanced round the other boxes, looking for

familiar faces. A young woman, two boxes below, waved to him and nudged her companion who raised a hand in salute. Hanson acknowledged the greeting and continued his scrutiny of the boxes. It was then that he saw the girl.

She would have been remarkable in any surroundings, but here, in the small group of matricians, she looked as out of place as a madonna in a brothel. Dark and slender with delicate features, she had an almost other-worldly look which suggested sensitivity and mysterious hidden depths. She was an image from days long past when women were delicate, shy creatures and men went out to fight for them. He could not imagine her fitting into the conventional pattern of domineering matriarchs and arranged marriages. But yet she had to. No woman who did not would be sitting in that box. He instinctively eyed the other people in the box, looking for her escort, for no matrician woman came unescorted to these matches. He picked him out easily—a tall fair-haired young man in the uniform of a lieutenant in the Matrician Guard. He had the arrogant bearing of one who was confident in his birth and physical qualities but had little else to recommend him. Hanson knew the type. Sons of matrician families who did not make the grade for the Administrative Service were given posts of this sort which carried all the privileges of their class but gave them only limited responsibilities, in this case ceremonial and escort duties coupled sometimes with police work. Their only chance of advancement was to marry into a powerful family.

He turned to look at the girl again. As if aware of his gaze she turned her head and their eyes met for a few seconds, Then she looked away quickly and began talking animatedly to her companion.

Hanson turned his attention to the pitch. The opposing teams were running out from the tunnel under the boxes to the accompaniment of cheers and flag waving from their supporters. Each team had a ball and for a few minutes they practised passing it to one another and shooting at the goals.

Then the referee ran out on to the pitch. He wore the usual black shirt and shorts. His head was protected by a padded metal helmet which was extended to cover his shoulders. Over his face was a grid of wire so thin as to be almost invisible, but strong enough to withstand the heaviest blow. Looped on one wrist was a whistle and on the other a short, but wicked-looking truncheon.

He blew his whistle and the practice stopped instantly. Eleven men took up their positions on either side of the pitch and another eight men from each team sat down on benches behind the goal posts. The cheering and shouting subsided and an expectant silence fell over the crowd. Hanson leaned forward to explain to Mashenko.

"This is a little different from the international game you have probably seen. The object is the same—to score as many goals as possible—but some of the rules have been changed. Each team is allowed eight reserves. A player can attack an opponent provided he is moving towards the ball. He is allowed to use his feet or his whole body, but not his hands. Kicking a man in the head is a major foul and the offender is removed from the game without a substitute being allowed."

The referee blew his whistle. The Tigers' centre-forward tapped the ball to the man on his left and immediately ran at the opposing centre, knocking him down. His partner kicked the ball into the gap and then the whistle blew.

"False start," Hanson said. "The other centre hadn't moved towards the ball—or at least the referee didn't think so," for an argument was going on in the centre of the pitch. The Tigers' centre shouted something at the referee who replied in kind. The centre raised his hand in a threatening gesture and the reprisal came so quickly that they almost didn't see it. Without his seeming to move, the referee's truncheon flashed briefly and the Tigers' centre-forward collapsed at his feet. From one end of the pitch came howls of rage and disappointment, from the other loud cheers of approbation. Two men rushed out from the sidelines and dragged away the unconscious man. As threatening the referee was a major foul, no substitute was allowed. This time it was the turn of the Chelsea Lions to kick off. Angry mutterings came from the Tigers' end of the pitch.

"This looks like being a lively game—they don't usually get worked up so early in the match."

The Lions' centre, a giant of a man, tried a different tactic. He tapped the ball towards the opposing centre who moved instinctively to kick it. The giant ran straight at him, hurling him to the ground and kicking the ball forward in the same movement. He made it for a few yards; then a smartly aimed kick, catching his foot just off the ground brought him crashing down. As he struggled to his feet a kick in the groin brought him down again. This time he did not get up.

"Wasn't that a foul?" Mashenko asked.

"Oh no, he actually took a step forward as he got up. That is enough to bring it within the rules. If he doesn't get up in two minutes he'll be taken off and a substitute put on."

The game was now a mass of players kicking and pushing on the Tigers' half-way line. Somehow or other the ball emerged and was booted up the field. The Lions' centre-forward was still lying where he had fallen and, where the scrimmage had been, another of their men was unconscious on the ground. As two orderlies ran out to drag away the injured centre, a substitute came running on. A minute or so later the unconscious man was hauled away and another substitute ran out.

Hanson explained, "The Tigers are one man short. Unless one of the other team attacks the referee or commits a major foul the only way they can win is to knock out more of their opponents than there are substitutes for. Sheer numbers can determine the winner. If no goals are scored, the team with the most players left at the end of the game are the winners."

By this time the crowd was on its feet, cheering and catcalling. In spite of himself, Mashenko was caught up and carried away in their excitement. He leaned forward and gripped the arms of his chair. The game swung to the centre line opposite their box. Matricians rarely showed excitement in public but a few of them, mostly women, were leaning forward in their seats. He glanced round at his companion. Hanson was sitting relaxed, his hands folded in his lap, his face completely devoid of expression. Only the cool grey eyes moved to follow the game. Mashenko had not noticed before how like his mother's they were.

Another scrimmage developed just below them. After a few moments the ball appeared at one side of it and one of the Lions who had been hovering on the outside swung his leg back to kick it. As he did so, one of the Tigers, who had also been waiting on the outside, kicked sharply upwards, catching him in the crutch. The man screamed in agony and rolled over, clutching himself. Mashenko closed his eyes in sympathetic agony and involuntarily squeezed his legs together.

Hanson glanced across at the girl. Her face was pale and she was sitting rigidly upright in her chair. He felt he would like to put his arms round her and protect her from he didn't know what. As if something of this had transmitted itself to her she turned round and looked him straight in the face, letting him see for a moment the distress in her eyes. Then, with a wry twitch of her lips she turned away again. At this point Hanson lost interest in the game. He followed it with his eyes but his mind was elsewhere. Twice in the next ten minutes their eyes met briefly. After the second time he turned round quickly and began talking to Mashenko.

By half-time the Lions were down to two reserves and the Tigers still had four. "I suppose you find this a little strange," Hanson remarked to Mashenko when the whistle had blown.

"Yes—very strange. Your mother said that women were

totally opposed to war and violence and yet they allow games like this. It does not make sense."

"As a matter of fact it makes very good sense. Women are realists—they accept that we are still in some ways largely animals and that men need outlets for their natural aggression. It is much better to let them work it off on the football pitch than to have it come out in ways which might be damaging to society. The real fun starts at the end of the match when the barriers are raised and the supporters fight it out on the pitch. No weapons are allowed—that way you get maximum aggression outlet with minimum damage."

"What about feet?"

"Haven't you noticed? All the Delta and Epsilon people are wearing special soft moccasins. They are not allowed in without them."

Midway through the second half the teams were equal. Each had ten men on the field and no reserves were left. Neither side had scored yet and the spectators were silent, waiting. Suddenly one of the Tigers got the ball. Four others formed a diamond-shaped cordon round him, one in front one behind and one on either side. As they raced up the pitch, the crowd got to its feet and roared. Two of the Lions' backs came charging up.

Hanson commented, "This is where it gets interesting. They can't attack the man in front because he is not running towards the ball, but he can attack them. Watch."

When the opposing backs were almost parallel with him, the man on the front of the diamond swerved at the last second and swept his leg round in a scything movement. The Lion back pitched forward on to his face. The man on the left of the diamond moved to intercept the cther back, but the Lion swerved and made for the man with the ball, the only one he could legitimately attack. The man on the right of the diamond ran at the back and they crashed head on into each other. Meantime the man with the ball raced towards the Lions' goal. One of the backs got up to his feet and tore after him, but a well-aimed kick brought him down again and this time he did not get up. The crowd at the Tigers' end of the pitch roared their approval. The goalkeeper moved out to intercept—a fatal mistake. The man with the ball tapped it to one side and brought him down with a hefty kick. Then he got to the ball again and gently dribbled it into the goal.

The crowd at the ends of the pitch were jumping up and down now. The Lions' blood was up. It was not enough now to cripple their opponents—they had to score at least one goal as well. The diamond trick would not work again. They had to use a different tactic. When the whistle blew the Lions' centre tapped the ball slightly forward and to the left. As the opposing centre moved instinctively towards it, he jumped and slammed him in the belly with both feet. Meantime the man on his left did the same for his opposite number. Together they raced up the pitch, swerving round their opponents and passing the ball from one to the other. They arrived, almost parallel, at the Tigers' goal and the goalkeeper, a heavily built man, hesitated for a moment, uncertain what to do, then moved forward a pace. The Lions left the ball and came straight at him. He didn't have a chance. With perfect timing one tripped him and the other jumped on his head as he was falling. As the jump had started before the man began to fall, the move was legal—but only just. Then one of them gently tapped the ball into the goal. The Tigers' supporters behind the goal howled with disappointment and shouted angrily at the referee, but he blew his whistle and signed for play to continue. Now they had one goal each and the Lions were one man up. The goalkeeper was unconscious, his face a bloody pulp, and moments later he was dragged away.

Now there was no pretence of caring about goals. They set out to cripple each other as quickly as possible. When the whistle blew for the end of the game the Lions were the undoubted winners. They had six men on their feet to their opponents' four and, to make doubly certain, they had managed to score another goal. The minute he had blown his whistle the referee sprinted for the exit, neatly dodging a kick aimed at him by one of the surviving Tigers. The barriers snapped up and, as the remaining players ran and limped to the exit, the crowds of supporters charged on to the pitch, knocking each other down in their frenzy to get to grips with the other side.

There were, in fact, no more than forty or fifty from either side, all men, running out on to the pitch. The remainder kept behind the goal lines, the women in front shouting encouragement. In seconds the pitch was a confused tangle of struggling bodies. To Mashenko it seemed that they were making more effort with their voices than with their fists. Gradually the mass crystallized into scores of individual conflicts, punching, kicking and hair-pulling.

Hanson looked across at the girl. She still looked pale and strained, but at the same time a little relieved. No serious damage would be done in this fighting. She was chattering quickly to her escort who was showing signs of being bored with this part of the performance. She glanced quickly at Hanson and as quickly back again, as if she regretted the unspoken intimacy of their previous exchanges. He wondered who she was and how he could get to know her. He did not recognize any of the people in her box—they belonged to what he called "the fun and games set"—women from good families and young men of no particular ability hoping to make advantageous marriages. He was conscious of a twinge of resentment—she deserved infinitely better than that.

An excited shout made him turn his attention back to the pitch. One of the Lions' supporters had his opponent down and was banging his head on the ground. A young woman who had come rushing out from behind the goal line was holding on to his hair, trying to pull him away. The man was desperately trying to shake her off.

"This should be interesting. He's not allowed to hit

her—if he does, he'll be arrested and sentenced to a public flogging."

The woman suddenly screamed, "He kicked me, he kicked me." Half a dozen uniformed guards ran out from below the Matrician boxes. Two of them seized the man and began to drag him away. A batch of Lions' supporters immediately relinquished their own battles and came to the rescue. Hanson could not afterwards describe accurately what happened next. More guards came out and more and more spectators turned to attack them. Within seconds what had merely been an amusing incident turned into an ugly situation. It looked almost as if it had been planned. The guards were clearly outnumbered. People in the Beta and Gamma seats began to leave. The Matricians sat tight. Then more supporters, seeing what was happening ran out on to the pitch. The women in the matrician boxes began to look anxious. Their men scrambled down to the front boxes, almost level with the pitch.

Mashenko turned nervously to Hanson. "What do we do now?"

"Stay where we are. Some of these men will be armed—we are not. I expect someone has sent for reinforcements."

Then it happened. A voice—Hanson could have sworn it was a woman's—called out from the pitch, "Down with the matricians—kill them, kill them." The cry was taken up by the crowd. "Kill them—kill the matricians." A group rushed towards the boxes. Mashenko started to his feet but Hanson put a restraining hand on his arm. "Don't move. By now they may have got to the exit and have us trapped."

Mashenko, whose scientific training had not taught him much about fighting or self-defence, would not sit down but stood looking from pitch to exit and back again. Hanson coolly surveyed the scene. Some of the men in front were armed with stun-ray guns which they were using effectively and unconscious bodies were beginning to pile up on the side line. But there were not enough of them—sooner or later some of the frenzied crowd would break through the cordon of fire. They could not hope to hold out for more than a few minutes if there were a break-through.

"We need some weapons. Help me smash the legs off this chair." Fortunately the chairs in the Matrician boxes were solid wooden affairs – a rare luxury in these days – and their combined efforts were enough to break off two sturdy legs, each with a jagged end. Hanson called out to the unarmed men in front and brandished his chair leg. They caught on and began smashing up chairs for themselves.

They were too late. Four of the supporters wearing rosettes in the Lions' colours, which had strangely remained in place during the fighting, slipped through a gap in the defenders and began clambering over the boxes. A tall matrician with a stun-ray turned to fire at them. He got one of them before he went down under a hail of blows from behind. The other three kept on coming. Hanson shouted to Mashenko and leapt over the rail into the next box. The girl was crouching, petrified, in one corner. Women in the other boxes began to scream. The attackers hesitated a moment when they saw the chair legs, then came on. The first one picked up a chair to act as a shield and advanced across the box below. When he got to the back of the box he raised the chair and jabbed it towards Hanson while his companions scrambled over the partition. Mashenko caught one of them a stunning blow with his chair leg but it was a clumsy weapon in the box cluttered with chairs. Before he could get a swing at the second one he had scrambled into the box and was making for the girl. Her scream brought Hanson whirling round. He dropped his improvised club and sprang at the man. A quick chop to the side of his neck dropped him neatly at the girl's feet. Hanson swung round, picked up a chair and hurled it straight into the face of the third man who was clambering over the partition.

Overhead, on the roof of the stadium, a siren began to wail. The rioters froze in their tracks then rushed frantically towards the ends of the pitch. As the first of them reached the seats behind the goals, the barriers slammed down. One man was trapped and screamed horribly for a brief instant. Those that remained on the pitch rushed around, beating frenziedly at the barriers and trying to escape through the tunnel leading to the dressing-rooms. The realization that there was no escape came to them slowly and the change that came over them was as frightening to Mashenko as their maniacal rage of a few minutes ago. They cowered terrified, huddled together as if for protection in the centre of the pitch. Some of them began wailing in hopeless terror.

Slowly the centre sections of the stadium roof slid apart to reveal two large heliplanes hovering above. As they gradually descended through the opening Mashenko could see armed police standing in the open hatchways. The crowd in the centre of the pitch began running round in frantic circles. When they got down to about ten feet the police opened up with their large automatic stun-rays, methodically sweeping the ground. In less than a minute there was no movement on the pitch. Huge nets dropped from hatches underneath the planes and police scrambled down them. As the planes touched the ground they spread the nets out and began piling bodies into them. They worked quickly and efficiently. Within ten minutes it was all over and the heliplanes were rising up through the roof, the nets dangling beneath them, full of unconscious bodies.

Absorbed by the masterly efficiency of the police operation, Hanson had forgotten about the girl. Now he turned to her. "Are you all right?"

"Yes, thanks to you. Those men would have killed me—I could see it in their eyes."

"What happened to your escort? He should have been with you."

"He got knocked out when they broke into the boxes—here he is now." Hanson looked round. The tall guardsman was making his way towards them through the tangle of overturned chairs. He moved stiffly and a bruise was beginning to form over one eye. Even in his battered condition he managed to maintain his air of confident arrogance. "Sorry," he grinned. "I was unavoidably detained, but I see you are quite safe."

She smiled impishly, "While you were playing soldiers, this gentleman saved my life." She turned to Hanson. "We had better introduce ourselves—I am Fiona Hamilton." Hanson turned to indicate Mashenko. "This is Nikolai Mashenko, Chief Physicist on the moon. My name is Hanson."

"Hanson? . . . that's strange . . . I . . ."

The guardsman broke in, "Hanson, did you say?" and then, with a slight touch of irony in his voice, "You are honoured—rescued by the only son of Baroness Alicia Hanson." He turned to Hanson, "My name is Lumsden—Alaric Lumsden. And now, if you will excuse us, I think I had better take Miss Hamilton home—she has had a very distressing experience."

With that he took her gently by the arm and led her unprotesting from the box. She turned to throw Hanson a look of gratitude and said, "I'll call you to-morrow."

As they left Mashenko said, "Well, you were right—the real excitement came when the game had finished. Does it often happen like that?"

"Never before, to my knowledge. I don't like it, Nikolai . . . there was something odd about it . . . almost as if it had been planned . . . I think it was a woman who gave the signal to attack."

"But why? Women are the masters—why should they want to upset the established order?"

"It's not as simple as that. Women like my mother rule the country, but that only applies at the very top. Further down the scale they have almost no say in what goes on. The women's liberation movement was essentially a middle-class intellectual affair. For the others it meant very little change. Theoretically and in law, they are superior to their menfolk, but I think some of them would be glad to go back to a . . . to the old ways." He had almost said, "to a more natural way of life."

"So—the matrician state is not all we are led to believe?"

"It works very efficiently, as you have just seen. We have not been engaged in a war for more than three generations and in that time our people have become the most prosperous in the world—and the most contented. That is why to-night's outbreak is so disturbing." He hesitated. "I have an appointment at ten-thirty to-morrow, but I would like to know what happens when these people appear in court to-morrow. Would you like to go and see British justice in operation?"

"But certainly. I have always wanted to see how your courts function. I've been told they are the fairest and the most efficient in the world."

Hanson permitted himself a grin. "We shall see . . . and now I think we had better be getting back—you have had quite enough excitement for your first night in London."

It was not until they walked into the living-room of the flat and found a scantily dressed young woman sitting on the couch sipping a drink that Hanson remembered his Stud Practice. He motioned the girl into his bedroom. "Will you excuse us for a moment?"

He turned to Mashenko who stood there goggling. "I'm sorry, I should have warned you. I had completely forgotten that I had ordered my stud practice for to-night."

Mashenko goggled even more. "Stud practice?"

"Yes, it is compulsory for all matrician men from the age of twenty-five. We are taught from the beginning that our purpose in life is to provide our wives with children and to ensure that they are sexually satisfied. You order a woman through the computer and each time it is recorded. If you fail to do it at least once a week the fact is noted on your record and can affect your chances of marriage and promotion. Your performance is reported on by the girl. To-night I am lucky—they have sent me an attractive young woman and I shan't have any problems. Sometimes they are ugly or old, or both—then it can be difficult."

"Now I understand why women of the lower classes want

to rebel. How long do you think this can go on?"

"Oh, I don't think these women are likely to rebel. Mostly they enjoy it and they live pampered lives compared with other women. Only matrician women have more luxurious existences—and they have to pay for it in much less pleasant ways. Their lives are much more restricted, hemmed in with all sorts of rules and taboos. One man a night is all that is asked of these girls. The rest of the time they are free to amuse themselves as they please—even to have lovers; and, as I said, they like it."

Mashenko shook his head. "I shall never understand it. In my country men and women fall in love and get married. They bring up their children together and respect each other. They don't look on their partners as breeding machines—or pleasure machines."

Hanson said, "I must not keep my examiner waiting. If there is anything you want, punch out the code on the computer terminal and it will be delivered to the service hatch."

"Is that how she came?" He nodded towards the bedroom.

"Yes, of course."

Once again Mashenko shook his head and said, "Terrible, terrible," and walked off muttering into his bedroom.

Hanson turned towards his bedroom door, then hesitated. His appetites were normal and healthy, but to-night, for some reason he had lost all his enthusiasm. It must have been that girl—Fiona. His mind lingered over the name. It would have to be Libidin, he decided. As a rule, Libidin tablets were prescribed only for married men, and then only at the wife's request, but he had managed to obtain a secret supply. There were times when even the best man could falter and it didn't pay to to risks with one's career. He went to the secret compartment in his desk, took out a tablet and swallowed it.

TWO

The atmosphere at breakfast was far from cordial and Mashenko remained silent through most of the meal. Apart from an enquiring glance round the living-room when he came through, he avoided the subject of the girl. After they had eaten Hanson wrote down directions for finding the criminal court and sent him on his way. His identity card had now been verified and he was free to visit the city on his own. They arranged to meet in the bar at the Richmond Gate.

When he had gone Hanson sat down at the computer terminal and keyed the Matrician Register. Blanchard's entry again came up as "No Record". Out of curiosity he tried his successor, Hughes. This time there was no question. It gave his appointment as a member of the Space Transport Committee along with the information that he was aged forty, the son of a former member of the Senate for South Wales, now retired, and had three elder sisters, all of whom were married.

This puzzled him—if Hughes's appointment had been gazetted, why not Tony Blanchard's? It was of course possible that someone had made a mistake—computers were only as accurate as the information fed into them. A careless operator might have accidentally erased Blanchard's entry while making the alterations. No doubt Hughes would be able to tell him something.

His next request to the computer was for Fiona Hamilton's entry in the Register. Within seconds it flashed on the screen.

Hamilton, Fiona. 2nd. d. of B. Mary Hamilton q.v.
Age 23. ed. Oxon. B.A. Hist. u/m.

The remaining details were lost on him. Absurd though it was on so short an acquaintance, he could not suppress a tiny thrill of excitement. An unmarried second daughter was a possible as far as his mother was concerned. Her mother's entry was also encouraging. She was chairman of several Senate committees, including the one for Space Transport and the influential Committee for Public Appointments.

As an afterthought he checked on her official escort. The answer was pretty much what he had expected. Lumsden was aged twenty-eight and had a married sister. His mother had held no public office of any kind, but his grandmother had been vice-chairman of the Senate. With this background he would be extremely lucky to marry the elder daughter of an influential family or even an obscure one. Competition in the breeding stakes was fierce. A second daughter with a small inheritance would be the most he could hope for. The mild dislike he had felt for the man the night before turned into something stronger.

At ten-thirty precisely Hanson was ushered into Hughes's private office in the Space Transport building. The only evidence that it was an office at all was a small desk, bare except for a visiphone and a single monitor screen. Otherwise it was a comfortable sitting-room such as one might find in any matrician house. There were several small couches, each with a table beside it, and a drinks cupboard partly open. One wall was a holovision telescreen. Hughes was standing in the window looking out over the landing area where the daily moon-shuttle was lifting off.

He turned round as Hanson came into the room. "There goes my day's work—not much, is it?"

Hanson did not quite know how to reply to that, but he was spared the embarrassment by the arrival of a tray of coffee.

Hughes was a small wiry man with dark hair beginning to recede from his temples. The eyes, which were also dark, gave the impression that they did not miss much and Hanson was uncomfortably aware of their scrutiny.

"I can guess what you have come for—two things—you are curious about my predecessor and you want to talk about transport arrangements for the moon."

In spite of himself, Hanson must have let the surprise show on his face. Hughes grinned, "I'm not clairvoyant—I have plenty of time to do my homework," and he gestured to the empty room.

"Let's take the easy one first. Thanks to our static society, I have fairly accurate traffic projections for the next five years. The only problem is venusium—I gather the demand is likely to be much higher than the original estimates—quite the wonder metal of the century, I'm told."

Hanson nodded and Hughes went on, "There is not enough money to enlarge the transit satellite or to build another one, but there is a cheaper solution. Most of the venusium will go to the manufacturing satellites—we shan't want much of it here on earth. At the moment your mining operations are producing about a million tons a year and sending it to Alpha One, but the accelerator you are using for launching it has a capacity of half as much again. If we get rid of the venusium that way the costs will be negligible and we can by-pass the transit satellite."

He went over to his desk and pulled out a folder which he handed to Hanson. "This is a copy of a detailed proposal which I have put to the Committee for discussion at the next full-scale meeting. I think you'll find I've covered everything."

Hanson glanced quickly through the papers. He had indeed covered everything. There were even figures allowing for the replacement of existing products by substitutes made from venusium.

He looked at Hughes with a new interest. The proposal was a masterpiece of concision and showed a grasp of the problem that would have been remarkable under any circumstances, but to have produced it within a few days of his appointment was little short of miraculous. Here was a man who, if only he had been married, should have been at the very top of the Service.

Hughes watched him with an amused smile, then his expression became serious.

"I'm afraid I can't help you with your other problem. Blanchard seems to have disappeared completely. I was given twenty-four hours to take over here and he had gone when I arrived. You know how it is when you take over a new job, there is always something you want to ask your predecessor. There was something I wanted to ask Blanchard and I called the Appointments Office after I had drawn a blank on the Register. They told me there was no way in which I could get in touch with him and, when I pressed the point, they made it clear, not in so many words, mind you, that it might be unhealthy to pursue the question any further."

He spread his hands in a gesture of resignation.

"What about the staff here?"

"They know nothing. He left at the usual time without saying anything and simply did not turn up next morning. The next thing they knew—I was here."

He got up and went to the drinks cupboard. "You'll join me in a drink?"

Hanson nodded. He wanted time to think—there had to be something he could do. As if reading his thoughts, Hughes said, "Of course, I was forgetting—you must have access to sources of information that are denied to the rest of us. Baroness Hanson can open a lot of doors." There was a touch of bitterness in the tone that made Hanson look at him sharply, but Hughes was smiling as if he were only too pleased to have found a solution.

Hanson sipped his drink slowly. His mother would almost certainly know, but, in that case, why had she not said anything? She must have known he would want to get in touch with Blanchard.

Hughes, still smiling, said, "I hear you were playing the

gallant knight yesterday."

"How did you hear that?"

"Oh, you know how news travels. That was quite a disturbance by all accounts. What did you make of it?"

"I don't know—there was something odd about it—almost as if it had been planned." He hesitated. This man seemed to have a finger on so many things—it might be worth while trailing his coat.

"I suppose you know about those messages that have been appearing in computer print-outs?" Hughes nodded. "I wondered if there might be a connection."

Hughes looked at him thoughtfully for a moment. "You take these messages seriously, then? I think they are probably a hoax—some kind of practical joke. Even if they aren't, I don't think there could be any connection with last night's riot. Who would try to start a revolution at a football match?"

Hanson set down his glass and got up to go. "By the way," he asked, "do you know a girl called Fiona Hamilton?"

Hughes shook his head. "I don't move in that set. I know of her—her mother is chairman of the Senate Space Transport Committee—a strange girl by all accounts—not at all what you would expect with a mother like hers. I've met her escort though—Guards officer called Lumsden—frustrated character." He paused. "Look here, I don't want to seem presumptuous, but . . . if you have any ideas in that direction, I should watch out for him. You know the type—they have a grudge against people like you and me."

As Hanson passed through the outer office a clerk in a Delta-class tunic who had been punching data into a computer terminal got up with a muttered excuse and left the room. Hanson smiled to Hughes's secretary and went out into the corridor. The little man was standing by the lift shaft. As Hanson approached he thrust a piece of paper in his hand and hurried off to the other end of the corridor where the toilets were.

Surprised, Hanson slipped the piece of paper into his

pocket and got into the lift. He would read it later when he was out of the building.

The Buckingham Bar was not very crowded when he got there — a few solitary individuals and one or two couples. He got himself a drink and settled down in a corner from which he could watch the door. Mashenko was to meet him here after he had been to the court. Hanson hoped he would find his way. The instructions had been clear, but one false digit punched on a railcar control panel could get him hopelessly lost. He took the piece of paper from his pocket. It was crudely printed in block letters except for the figures which were neatly written. The message was simple — and mystifying,

"COME TO 063 2451 TONIGHT 2100"

Hanson slipped the note back into his pocket and sipped his drink thoughtfully. It could only concern Blanchard. The man must have recognized him from a previous visit.

The bar was slowly beginning to fill as people drifted in from the walk-way outside. Hanson, scanning the doorway, recognized a casual acquaintance who came over to greet him.

His name was Mitchell. Hanson did not know him well. They had sat together on a number of committees during their early days in the Service and had struck up an acquaintanceship which had continued in a desultory sort of way long after their careers had taken diverging paths. Mitchell was primarily a mathematician and specialized in astro-physical computing systems. He was not ambitious. He enjoyed his work and had not bothered to marry. His life was pleasant and interesting and he saw no reason to burden himself with responsibilities which would only interfere with his pleasures,

"Heard you were back — rescuing damsels in distress and all that."

"It was only a little scuffle. Were you there?"

"No. I met Fiona Hamilton this morning, bubbling over with tales of a gallant knight rushing to her rescue. You've made a hit there all right . . . not that she's my cup of tea . . . too thin and starry-eyed. I prefer something with more meat on it. Anyway, that fellow Lumsden won't let anyone near her."

Hanson was pleased but tried not to show it. He kept the conversation on the same bantering plane.

"We administrators like to flex our muscles occasionally to show what good all-rounders we are. We have simple pleasures. We don't translate our women into mathematical formulae."

Mitchell had once occupied the whole of a rather dull meeting in reducing to an algebraic formula the curve of a buxom secretary's hips.

"What was that riot all about last night? . . . I heard a rumour that it was triggered off by a woman."

"Hard to say. I got the distinct impression that it was a woman's shout that started the attack on our boxes, but I couldn't be sure. There was a lot of shouting going on at the time."

"Not this Malib thing, then?"

"Malib?—Do you know anything about it?"

"Oh, one hears rumours. Storm in a teacup I shouldn't wonder. Can't imagine anyone taking it seriously. From what little sociology I've read men have much more freedom now than they ever had in the old days. No wives to support and no responsibility for bringing up children. Let the women have the problems—I'm quite happy as I am."

At that moment Mashenko came through the door, obviously bursting to tell him something. Hanson made a warning sign and introduced him to Mitchell. After a few polite pleasantries Mitchell wandered away to join some friends at the bar. Hanson signed to a waiter and ordered a drink for Mashenko.

"Well, and how did you find British justice?"

Mashenko swallowed his drink—neat vodka—at one gulp, and leaned forward, his elbows on the table.

"It was certainly efficient—but very strange. I didn't understand some of what went on. There was a woman judge, but no jury or witnesses. A man whom I took to be the prosecutor handed the judge a document which she read very quickly. Then they projected some photographs on to a large screen at the back of the court. Another man, who seemed to be the defence counsel was given a copy of the document. He did not read it at all.

"When all the photographs had been projected the judge simply turned and looked at the defence counsel who nodded his head. Then the prisoners were brought in one at a time. Each was shown the photograph in which he appeared and then he was sentenced."

"What were the sentences?"

"That was strange too. They were all let off except ten men and one woman. I didn't understand the sentence. The judge simply said, "Game Park," and signed a paper. What did that mean? They were terrified. Some of them struggled and had to be dragged away."

Hanson glanced at his watch and got to his feet. "We have just time to visit the Game Park if you don't mind a late lunch. I'll explain it on the way."

Hanson cut the heliplane's rotor and opened the lateral jets when it reached two thousand feet.

"You wondered why only some of the prisoners were sentenced?" Mashenko nodded and he went on, "It is a practice that dates back a long time—to the end of the twentieth century, in fact, when this country was plagued by outbreaks of vandalism and mob violence. There were not enough prisons to accommodate all those who were arrested and there was no money to build any more. The government of the time found an effective answer. The death penalty was introduced for murder and flogging for other crimes of violence, but these penalties were only applied at random, and only when proof of guilt was established beyond doubt. Now and again selected criminals were hanged or flogged and imprisoned. As selection was random and there was no right of appeal against sentence, no-one taking part in a crime knew whether he would get the maximum sentence. Prison treatment was savage—inadequate diet and flogging for the least offence. Within two years, crimes of violence had almost disappeared. A few executions, public floggings and harsh prison sentences were enough. Since then we have continued the practice of occasional severe and random punishment for all crimes. It is cheap and effective."

"What about the Game Park?"

"You'll see it in a moment—there it is ahead of us now."

Hanson switched on the rotor and guided the plane down towards a white building, flat-roofed, with solar collectors at each end of it. From either side of the building, as far as the eye could see, there ran a fence which Mashenko judged to be at least forty feet high. The country beyond it was thickly wooded as was most of what they had passed over, but there the similarity ended. There were no buildings to be seen nor any patches of cultivated ground, only rough clearings here and there among the trees.

They landed on the roof and when Hanson explained their purpose they were led into the Deputy Warden's office. A tall, heavily built woman got up to greet them. Her age was difficult to determine, but Mashenko judged her to be in her late thirties. Her straight blonde hair was cut short and the face was strong and masculine with a heavy square jaw. Hanson explained that he wanted to fly over the park and show it to his guest.

"No private planes are allowed over the Park now—there have been too many low-flying accidents. The new regulations came into force a week ago. May I see your cards, please."

They produced them and, after studying Mashenko's carefully, she glanced at Hanson's. Her expression changed and her overbearing stance became subtly respectful.

"I'm sorry, sir, I cannot make any exceptions, nor can the Warden, but if you wait a moment I'll go and speak to her."

When she returned she said, "The warden has no power to make an exception, but she will put one of the patrol craft at your disposal and the pilot will take you where you want. We've sent a message to the nearest one. It will be here in about ten minutes."

They went up to the roof to wait for it. A large passenger heliplane had just landed. The doors opened and a guard stepped out, her stun-ray at the ready. A stream of prisoners emerged. They were all clad in bright orange one-piece overalls and each had a white circle on his back with a number on it. They wore belts with sheath knives dangling from them. There was one woman dressed in the same garb.

Mashenko exclaimed, "These are the people I saw in court this morning—the rioters from the football match."

"Yes, I thought we might see them. They don't waste much time after sentencing. Their details will be checked here to see that they agree with the information sent on from the court, and in half an hour at the most they will be flown out to the park and set down, each in a different place."

"What happens then?"

"They live on the small game in the park, if they can catch it. That is their real punishment. None of these people have eaten animal flesh in their lives and they have been conditioned to make the idea revolting to them. They would almost as soon eat each other." He grinned. "Only we barbarous matricians eat animals."

"How long do they stay in the park?"

"Only six months. After that they are automatically released. Not all of them want to be released. Those who survive and adapt themselves sometimes prefer to stay on. After all, it is a more natural way of life than being cooped up in a city like a lot of automatons. I believe there are small colonies here and there. We don't know much about them—the park is too overgrown for them to be seen from the air and it is not safe to land. The only people who risk going in on foot are the hunters in the autumn—and some of them disappear every year. The convicts probably kill them to get their weapons. A knife is not the best equipment for catching game. Released prisoners tell stories of small tribes with savage leaders and constant fighting over the limited supply of women. These are probably exaggerated, but there must be some basis of truth in them."

Mashenko shook his head in lugubrious bewilderment. It was becoming almost a characteristic gesture.

A patrol heliplane landed on the roof and the pilot, a woman, came towartds them and saluted.

"First Officer Wilson, sir. Where would you like to go? We have an hour before I come off duty."

"My friend here would like to see the park—some of the game, if you can show us any—and, of course, some convicts."

"That may not be so easy, sir. Game perhaps, but convicts . . . that is another matter. I haven't seen one all morning. They hide when they see us coming. There may be a chance if we fly over the release collection point. The next batch of releases is due in a week's time and some of them ought to be making their way there now."

Mashenko looked at her with interest. So far most of the women he had seen in similar jobs had been singularly unattractive, but this girl was different. Small and neatly built, with jet black hair, she was almost beautiful. Only the nose, which was straight and a shade too long, marred the symmetry of her features.

Mile upon mile of forest rolled beneath them as they flew slowly northwards. Occasionally they passed over areas where the vegetation was sparse and scrubby and where a few mouldering remnants of buildings could be seen.

"These were once towns," Hanson explained. "That one over there was Leicester. It was abandoned a long time ago."

The heliplane slowed and began to lose height. Ahead of

them, standing on a piece of high ground surrounded by rocky outcrops, was a small building. Mashenko noticed that there were no solar collectors on the flat roof.

"The Collection Centre," their pilot explained, as she cut the jets and let the rotor take over. "We'll do a few circles round the area to see if we can spot any convicts. The warnings have been out for nearly two weeks now and some of them should be in the neighbourhood."

They circled the area slowly but saw no sign of life until a deer suddenly bounded out into a clearing and collapsed. "We've got one," the pilot said. "Can you see the arrow?"

A strange looking creature broke from the undergrowth and ran towards the stag. It took Mashenko a moment to realize that he was looking at a man. His head and most of his face were covered with hair and he wore a garment roughly fashioned from animal skins. He seized the stag and began to drag it away. Two more figures, equally strange, appeared from the other side of the clearing and jumped on him. After a brief struggle, they made off with the deer, leaving the first man lying on the ground.

"I'm going to teach those two a lesson," said the girl and brought the heliplane over the clearing with a burst of the jets that jerked her passengers back in their seats. Too late, the men saw it, dropped the deer and began to sprint for the trees. She flicked a switch and, almost instantly, the two convicts clapped their hands to their ears and ran about in frantic circles. She adjusted a control and they fell to the ground twisting and kicking, their hands still pressed to their ears. "High frequency sound," the girl explained. "If I keep it up long enough it will drive them insane."

Mashenko had heard of uni-directional sonic waves but this was the first time he had seen them in action. No sound at all came to those in the heliplane.

They landed in the clearing and First Officer Wilson jumped out brandishing her stun-ray. "You are going to pay for this. The state has no room for parasites who prey on other people's work. I'm going to take your numbers and report you to the Warden. Your sentences will start again from to-day." She calmly pointed her stun-ray at them and they collapsed unconscious to the ground. After examining their wrists she made a note and went over to their victim who was struggling to his feet. "You had better take your deer and get well away from here before those two come round." The man muttered something, grabbed the stag by the legs and dragged it from the clearing.

Back in the plane she said, "I may not have done him any good." She looked at her note pad. "Those two were due to be released next week — now they have another six months to do. They will probably kill him if he is still about when they come round."

"Why weren't they wearing their orange-coloured uniforms?" Mashenko asked.

"They discard these as soon as they can get hold of some skins — they are too conspicuous for hunting in. Their numbers are tattooed on their wrists so that they can be checked when they come up for release. At one time they used to be punished if they were caught out of uniform, but it soon became impossible and we stopped trying."

They took off and continued to fly low over the park using the sonic beam to flush out game. Mashenko was fascinated at the variety. There were several sorts of deer, pheasants, partridges, foxes, wild pigs and, once, a herd of wild cattle, great shaggy beasts with wicked looking horns. They saw no more convicts until they were on their way back, when they came across the large passenger heliplane in a clearing. An orange-clad figure was pushed out and the plane took off again. The convict looked around him quickly, as if to get his bearings, and then set off through the forest at a determined pace.

"That's odd," the girl said. "As a rule, when they are first put down they hang about for a long time, not knowing where to go or what to do. That one looked as if he knew where he was going."

"What will happen to the woman?" Mashenko asked.

"She will be put down with one man to protect her. If he is strong he may be able to keep her; if not, the first man they meet will try to take her from him and kill him if he resists. That is what usually happens. The men who have been in the park for some time are obviously fitter and desperate for a woman. For a man to be set down with a woman is almost certain death unless he gives up and runs away."

For a moment an expression of sheer hatred came over her features. "They are the worst of all—these women who let their sex down. If I had my way they would be raped a hundred times and then killed."

Mashenko said nothing, but stared with a set face through the canopy. What shocked him most was that this woman could be so cold-blooded and savage, and yet at the same time was so feminine and attractive. Had he met her anywhere else he might have found himself fancying her.

Back in the flat that afternoon after they had finished lunch, Mashenko stood staring sombrely through the window.

"There are so many things I don't understand in your country—all that wasted land, for example—hundreds of square miles used for a prison,"

"The land isn't wasted. You saw for yourself the variety of wild life it supports. The convicts are merely incidental. For centuries we exploited the land, digging out minerals and farming it with chemicals. Some parts near the east coast are only now emerging from the desert our ancestors created.

"Once synthetic proteins became cheap and almost indistinguishable from real meat, we discovered that we could feed our population, and to spare, without plundering the land. Farming became uneconomical and people drifted to the cities where life was easy and no man had to work more than half of each day. Only we matricians have preserved the old ways—we still live off the land and hunt game, but only on a small scale. My father spends an hour or so a day running the London heliplane factory by remote control. The rest of his time he devotes to farming the estate, rearing cattle and horses. There is plenty for everyone and the land is preserved—no farming, no mining, no pollution."

"That is all very nice for you—but what about all the people shut up in the towns with no say in what goes on?"

"They are happy enough—plenty food, leisure and entertainment and not too much work. You can't have democracy and a stable society—you must sacrifice one or the other. Anyway, this is no time for philosophizing. You are here to enjoy yourself. I have an urgent appointment this evening so I have arranged an entertainment for you."

"After last night I am not sure that I like your entertainments. Who is going to be killed or maimed to-night?"

"No-one. You are going to a party—music, dancing, wine such as you have never tasted and a beautiful girl to introduce you to it."

"Why do you have urgent appointments when you are on leave? . . . The girl at the football match?"

"I wish it were. Nothing so pleasant—a piece of tiresome private business I have to attend to."

"This girl—she is coming from the computer?"

"No, I promise you—a beautiful young matrician lady—she may surprise you."

The visiphone buzzed and Mashenko had to be content with that. Hanson switched it on and Fiona Hamilton appeared on the screen. She looked, if anything, more desirable than she had last night.

"Can you come to see me? It is not just to thank you for saving my life last night . . . there is something else we have to talk about . . . but in private."

"I have an appointment this evening, but I am free to-morrow." He glanced at Mashenko. "I think the morning would be best."

"Come to my mother's house at ten." He nodded assent and she flashed him a brief smile before switching off. She had seemed strangely anxious. Then he remembered that she had been on the point of saying something the night before when Lumsden had dragged her off.

Mashenko's hostess for the evening arrived to pick him up after dinner. A tall red-head, bursting with energy, she took command the moment she entered the flat. Her dress, which only just complied with the regulation style, was cut to make the most of her ample charms. She greeted Hanson effusively, taking his chin in her hands and kissing him on both cheeks.

"How nice to see you again."

She turned to Mashenko. "So this is your Russian friend. You must be dying for a taste of civilization after being shut up on the moon for months. I'm told things are different in Russia. It will be nice to introduce you to your first English party."

Hanson grinned. He was not altogether sure he had done the right thing. Leonora Fallon was notorious, even for these enlightened days when matrician women had much more freedom than they used to have. Her mother had been killed in an accident when she was quite young and, right from the start, she had more freedom than was usually allowed to matrician girls. She had been married off to a nonentity whose mother had been sufficiently influential to prevent him being sterilized—the usual fate of matrician men who did not come up to the minimum standard of intelligence. Rumour had it that she kept him shut up in her country house and only called on him when no other man was available.

When they had gone, Hanson glanced at his watch. It was almost time to go. He went to his wardrobe and took out a Delta-class tunic, a relic of his training days. All members of the Administrative Service had to spend three months as a semi-skilled Delta, sharing their accommodation and doing an appropriate job. Hanson's job had been as a production worker in his father's heliplane factory. He opened his own tunic and slipped the flimsy grey one inside it, wrapping it round his chest. That done he hesitated a moment, then took from the secret compartment in his desk a small black metal tube which he fitted into a specially prepared pocket inside his trouser fly. A perfunctory search would reveal no more than that he was particularly well equipped in that area.

At exactly nine o'clock he pushed the button on the door of Delta Living Module 063 2451. Earlier, in a public washroom at the railcar terminal, he had switched tunics and now wore the grey insignia of the semi-skilled worker. The door was opened by the little man he had seen at the Space Transport office who gave him a dismayed look, then glanced along the corridor and beckoned him inside.

"I'm sorry, sir, I didn't recognize you in that tunic—one has to be careful."

Hanson looked about him with interest. The room was larger than the one he had occupied during his training, but he was surprised at the sparseness of the furnishings—a few easy chairs, a couch and some cheap ornaments. A woman was stretched out on the couch, her eyes glued to the holovision screen which occupied most of one wall.

"This is my wife, Anna—our name is Munn. Anna dear, this is the Mr Hanson I told you about."

The woman got up. Her features were pallid and drawn and Hanson could see that she was pregnant.

"Coffee?" she asked, and when Hanson nodded, she went through to the service module which had a doorway but no door. Through it he could see the eating bench and narrow stool moulded in one piece with the floor. Above the bench was the delivery hatch and on the opposite wall, he assumed, were the waste disposal chutes, one for organic materials and one for inorganic. Next to it was the bathroom which had a door and shared the organic waste chute, connected through a series of ducts to the recycling unit which served each block of five hundred modules.

Munn, who seemed nervous, went over to the holovision screen and turned down the volume. He motioned Hanson to one of the chairs and apologized for the scanty furnishings. "Anna and I have been selected to have a daughter and we are saving our credits so that she can have the best of everything."

The woman returned with two beakers of synthetic coffee which she set down beside the men.

"Aren't you having one yourself, my dear?"

She shook her head. "I spend all day drinking cups of this stuff and watching the holoscreen. It always tastes the same and the programmes are all the same too. I shall be glad when this is over and I can get back to work again. You men still have the best of it. You don't have to sit around all day with a swollen body and nothing to do but think about it."

Munn glanced nervously at Hanson. "You must excuse Anna, sir. This is our first child and she is finding it difficult—she doesn't even let me wait on her as I used to."

The woman picked up a packet of Tranquillo cigarettes and lit one. Then she went over to the holoscreen and turned the volume up slightly. Munn opened his mouth as if to protest but thought better of it. She lay down on the couch again and became wholly absorbed in what appeared to be a bedroom drama in which an incredibly handsome matrician was about to seduce an equally attractive Delta girl.

Munn said apologetically, "We had better go into the sleeping room, sir. It will be quieter there," and he led Hanson through the door. The sleeping module was almost as bare as the one they had just left, but some effort had been made to brighten it up. A vase of artificial flowers, resembling nothing Hanson had ever seen growing anywhere, stood on a ledge. Two more, similarly burdened, stood on either side of the small dressing-table and the chair, the only movable piece of furniture in the room, had a cushion made of some bright red material. The dressing-table was untidy. Tubes and pots, some opened, were scattered over its surface and an ashtray overflowed on to an open packet of Tranquillo cigarettes.

Munn sat down on the bed. "I'm not quite sure where to begin, sir. I expect you are wondering what it is all about. It's Mr Blanchard, sir he asked me to get in touch with you . . . if anything should happen. You see, Mr Blanchard was a very efficient gentleman and quite often there was no work for us to do and then he would talk to me sometimes. He was very kind—always seemed interested in how I lived and what sort of things I did and thought about. We got quite friendly, you might say and once he even came here to have some coffee with us. Not at all like what you would expect from a matrician."

He paused and looked at Hanson as if he expected him to tell him what to say next.

"The night before he . . . went away, he called me into his office when everyone had gone. He said that he was doing something that might be dangerous and that one day he might not show up at the office. If that happened I was not to ask about him. It might be dangerous, he said, if anyone was to try to find out about him. Then he said, sir, that you might enquire about him and if you did I was to give you a message."

"What message?"

Munn hesitated, "I couldn't understand it, sir. He just said tell him the moon is the key."

"Nothing else?"

"No, sir. I asked him because I couldn't understand it and he said he didn't want you to try to find him but if you were really determined to do it you would be able to work it out for yourself."

"You are quite sure there was nothing else? Did he say anything to you at any other time that seemed strange to you?"

"A lot of what he said seemed strange to me, sir, and a lot of it went over my head."

He hesitated a little as if searching for something. "There was one thing, though. I didn't think much about it at the time, but it kind of stuck in my head—different from the usual kind of thing he used to ask me. He asked me if I had ever heard of something called . . . it was a strange name . . . sounded like mal—something."

"Malib?"

"Yes—that was it—Malib. He said if I ever heard anything to let him know, but not to mention it to anyone else."

"And did you?"

"No, sir, I never did."

"Did Mr Blanchard ever talk to you about himself or mention anyone he had been seeing?"

"He never talked about himself. He seemed more interested in me and what people like me were thinking."

Hanson got up to go. There was nothing more to be learned here. Munn's wife was still totally absorbed in the holoscreen as he passed through the room and made no acknowledgement of his going. He noted that the pair on the screen had got into bed together and suggestive movements were taking place underneath the blanket.

The bar at the Richmond Gate was beginning to fill up when he arrived. He got himself a drink and looked round for somewhere to sit. A voice greeted him from behind, "What have you done with your Russian friend to-night?" He turned round to find Lumsden regarding him with a sardonic smile. "Mashenko?—he's gone to a party. I had something to do this evening."

"Gone to a party?—you do your entertaining painlessly—party to-night and court this morning."

Hanson raised an eyebrow. "Were you there then?"

"We Guards do have some duties besides escorting young ladies. By the way, talking of young ladies—I must apologize for taking my charge away before she had time to thank you properly."

"No need to apologize—I shall be seeing her in the

morning."

It was Lumsden's turn to raise an eyebrow. "To-morrow, eh? That's strange—she told me she wouldn't need an escort to-morrow." There was a tinge of suspicion in his tone.

"I'm seeing her at her mother's house—she doesn't need an escort there."

Lumsden's eyes narrowed. He was clearly put out by this piece of information. Hanson finished his drink quickly and took his leave. He was conscious of Lumsden's eyes boring into his back all the way across the bar.

THREE

There was no sign of Mashenko in the morning and his bed had not been slept in. He was not really surprised. Most of the men in Leonora's circle were wary of her by now and she was always on the look-out for new blood. Mashenko, with his Slav romanticism and his streak of puritanism would be a new experience for her. With any luck she would keep him out of the way for the rest of the morning.

He sat down to a leisurely breakfast with the morning's copy of the *Matrician News*. On the front page there was an account of the fracas at the football match, sandwiched between a report of a fashionable wedding and a polo match. It contained only a bald statement of the facts—that there had been a disturbance at the match and that the offenders had been arrested and dealt with. Nothing was said about the attack on the matrician boxes, nor was there any mention of the woman on the pitch. The authorities had obviously decided to play the whole thing down—that meant they must be worried about it.

When he had finished breakfast he went over to the visiphone and keyed the number of Leonora's flat. There was a short delay before the screen snapped on and a tousle-headed Leonora squinted at him through half opened eyes.

"Oh, it's you. What a time to wake anyone. If it's Nikki you want, he's sound asleep and I'm not going to disturb him. The poor man has earned his rest, and besides, I haven't finished with him yet. I'll bring him back this evening."

With that she switched off. Hanson smiled. Mashenko had evidently fallen from his pedestal of virtue.

An hour later his heliplane whirred to a halt on the landing-pad of the Hamilton house. It was smaller than his mother's but the estate was quite large as far as he could judge from the perimeter fence which stretched for several miles round it. Fiona was waiting for him at the door and led him upstairs to a small sitting-room looking out on to a part of the garden which had been allowed to run wild. Trees, shrubs and flowers jostled one another with scarcely a path between them. Here and there, through the trees, he caught a glimpse of water.

"My private wilderness," she said, "where no-one goes but me. There hasn't been a gardener in it for five years."

Hanson looked round the room and noted with satisfaction that there were a large number of books on the walls. Apart from a collection of modern historical works, there was a fair sprinkling of poetry and old novels, some in their original bindings. Most people, these days, even matricians, relied on their holoscreens for entertainment and got any information they needed from small computers arranged by subjects. It was perfectly possible to lead a useful life without ever opening a book.

She ordered coffee and sat down motioning him to a chair. She was simply dressed in the standard tunic and trousers which showed her slim figure to advantage. Looking at her now, face to face for the first time, he saw that she was, if anything, even more attractive than she had seemed at the football match. There was a sort of elfin quality about her that he found difficult to define and, when she smiled, her features took on an almost impish expression. She smiled at him now as the manservant set down a tray laden with a silver coffee-pot and delicate, hand-painted porcelain cups.

When the man had left the room she said, "I didn't just ask you here to thank you—though I couldn't do that enough—there is something else." Her face became serious. "It's about Tony Blanchard—you know he has disappeared?"

Hanson nodded. If he was surprised he did not allow it to show on his face and she went on, "It's all so vague . . . I don't know quite where to begin. It was something he said the last time I saw him—something about getting in touch with you if anything should go wrong. I can't remember his exact words, but I think he said that you would be able to work it out if you talked with me—oh, and there was another thing—he said to let you know that he had discovered something odd about the prisoners being sent to the moon." She flung out her hands in a gesture of puzzlement and sat back in her chair. "Do you know where he is?"

Hanson shook his head. "I got another message last night—from a clerk in the Space Transport Office. It was also a bit vague."

"What was it?"

"Simply that the moon was the key."

Fiona looked more mystified than ever and Hanson sipped his coffee reflectively. One thing was plain. Blanchard thought it was too dangerous to impart specific information and too dangerous even to let one person have all his clues. Years ago, when he was still at school, Blanchard used to amuse him by setting him puzzles. He would give him one cryptic clue and leave him to find the others for himself. Sometimes it would take him weeks of piecing together tiny scraps of information before he found the answer, but he always knew when he had found it. The logic of the correct solution was inescapable and perfectly clear. There could be no other answer. It looked rather as if he had set him another puzzle—only this time it was serious—perhaps deadly serious. He grinned wryly at the pun and said to Fiona, "I think this may take a long time," and he explained about Blanchard's games.

"I'm not sure that I like being a sort of walking crossword clue. Where do we start?"

"Right back at the beginning—when you first met him."

"That was about a year ago. He came to Oxford to give a

talk on the effects of transport systems on the evolution of societies. At the end of the talk he asked for questions. I asked one that was a little complicated and he invited me to have coffee with him in the Common Room when the others had gone. He had some interesting theories about the invention of the internal combustion engine and the aeroplane—thought they were largely responsible for the break-up of society at the end of the twentieth century. I didn't agree with everything he said and we argued about it.

"After that we saw quite a lot of each other. At first we just talked about history, but later we just enjoyed one another's company. You see, I could feel at ease with him because the sex thing didn't arise. He was almost, I suppose, what used to be called fatherly. I often thought he would have been happier teaching in a university than as an administrator. He didn't seem to have much ambition."

"Did he talk much about himself?"

"Hardly ever. I don't know what he did when he wasn't with me. He seemed to spend a lot of his time just thinking and reading. From time to time he would borrow a book from me—mostly history texts."

"Tell me about the lecture."

"I can't remember every detail of it. His main argument was that historians in the past had paid too little attention to the effect of transport methods on the development of society. He didn't so much propound a theory as point out a few things and suggest possible lines of research. At first I was inclined to pooh-pooh it—transport was his job after all and he naturally exaggerated its importance.

"But afterwards I began to get interested. He believed that the motor car and the aeroplane helped to accelerate the social discontent at the end of the twentieth century; that they changed people's lives so quickly that they had no time to adjust to them. It was no longer an adventure to visit another town—or even another country. When travel was the prerogative of the rich it didn't matter much, but once cheap transport was available to everyone and the ordinary citizen could travel anywhere he liked at very little cost, then he became discontented. There were no new frontiers to cross, except one. He attacked the Establishment.

"This seemed to be a little far-fetched but there were some facts which seemed to support it. Our records for that period are not good enough for us to be certain about the real causes. People then had only the haziest notions about historical change and the things they thought important to record had very little bearing on what was actually happening. It was only when women took over and stopped people tampering with things they didn't understand that we got a return to stability."

She stopped talking and looked at him questioningly.

"Is this getting anywhere?"

"I think it might. Did he say anything about control of transport to-day?"

"Yes. He thought that we had become too dependent on space transport for our supplies of raw materials and manufactured goods."

Hanson got up. "May I use your visiphone?" She nodded and he went over to it and keyed his mother's private number. There was no reply. He keyed another number and immediately the face of her confidential secretary appeared on the screen.

"Yes, Mr Hanson?"

"My mother not there?"

"No, she's in Germany but I expect her back this afternoon."

"Tell her I'm coming down and would like to see her." He snapped the switch off to forestall any objection and turned to Fiona.

"I think my mother has some explaining to do—she must know where he is."

"I thought my mother would know, but she refused to discuss it. There is something very strange going on."

She pushed a button and the manservant appeared to clear away the coffee-tray. "If you have time before you go I would like to show you my garden."

Afterwards, sitting on a rock beside a small stream, "This is where I come when I want to be alone . . . it is so peaceful . . . so natural." He was no botanist but he had noticed that all the trees and plants, as far as his untutored eye could judge, were the original species. There was no trace of the geneticist's curiosities that were fashionable for the moment. Prevented by international legislation from practising on human beings, the geneticists turned their attention to animals and plants and people vied with one another in having new and fantastic creations in their gardens—jet black roses a foot in diameter, brilliant red daffodil bushes, edible tulips with crisp sweet petals and a host of other strange plants. Here, in this quiet spot, there were none of these monstrosities. Wild and tangled though it was, it held a sense of peace and natural harmony that was not to be found in the acres of orderly extravaganzas that made up most matrician gardens.

"It's a pity that all this will be destroyed one day."

He looked at her questioningly.

"My sister Mary. One day she and her husband will come to live here and they will make it like the rest of the grounds. She likes everything to be tidy and controlled."

"That would be a shame, but you can always have another one somewhere else."

"It wouldn't be the same. This place has so many memories. When I was sad, I used to come here to be consoled and when I was particularly happy, I came here too. Mary used to laugh at me and say I was born a thousand years too late—I should have lived in an age when ladies stayed at home and their knights went out to do battle for them. She may have been right. There are times when I feel that ours is not a natural way of life."

Suddenly, as if conscious that she had said too much, she stood up.

"You must go now. The servants will be getting

suspicious."

Hanson felt as if he had been rebuffed, that she regretted having revealed something of her inner self to him. Her face had assumed its impenetrable matrician mask.

Half way up the path she stopped, put a warning hand on his arm and pointed towards a bush that was performing curious rhythmic movements. Motioning him to silence, she stepped quietly and carefully towards it. What he saw almost made him laugh aloud. Struggling on the ground behind the bush were two bodies clad in Epsilon tunics, but without their trousers. The man twisted his head round and looked at them, fear in his eyes. The woman tried to cover her face with her hands. Fiona flushed angrily, drew back her elegant foot and kicked twice with all her strength. The man winced, but made no sound.

"You know you are not allowed in here. Get back to the house at once." With a final kick she strode back to the path. Her cheeks were still flushed, but now it was with embarrassment.

"I'll have them whipped for that."

They walked back to the house in silence. Hanson was afraid to say anything that might bring back her anger. When they reached the landing-pad she stopped.

"I think we had better say good-bye here. Will you get in touch with me when you have seen your mother?"

"This evening. Where will you be?"

"At the flat."

With that she turned on her heel and went towards the house. Hanson, piqued at this curt dismissal which seemed so out of character, watched her retreating back a moment, then climbed into his machine. As he cleared the trees he saw two brown-clad figures slinking timidly towards the house.

High above the Hamilton estate a heliplane circled lazily. It was painted a pale blue which, at that height, made it almost invisible from the ground. Its rotor was turning too fast to be seen, but it also was painted blue. The pilot had been up there for more than an hour now and he was beginning to get bored. From time to time he glanced at his teleview screen which was focused on the landing-pad in front of the house. At last a movement on the pad aroused a flicker of interest in his eyes. He watched Hanson's machine take off and then, keeping above and behind it, he followed. Ten minutes later, satisfied about its destination, he swung the plane round and headed at high speed towards London.

The baroness was in her office and could not be disturbed, the secretary told him. Yes, she had been told of his call and would send for him when she was free. This was not his day for succeeding with women, he reflected. What he needed right now was some male company. He knocked at the door of his father's office and went in.

David Hanson (né Collins) in his sixties still retained a look of boyish good humour. He looked up cheerfully from one of the monitor screens on his desk and waved a greeting.

"Won't be long—must settle this before lunch."

Several sets of figures were displayed on the screen. Some of them remained the same while others changed at varying speeds. His father pointed to one of them. "These stabilizer control panels are lagging behind again." He pushed a button and a section of the heliplane plant appeared on another screen. There were four machines, three of them apparently working and the fourth stripped down on a bench. Two Gamma technicians were bending over it. He adjusted the controls to get a close-up. The two men were examining some metal parts on the bench and one of them wore a puzzled expression. He watched them closely for a moment then keyed a number on the factory visiphone. The worried face of the production manager appeared on the screen.

"Trouble on those stabilizer panels again, I see."

"Yes, sir. This is the second time to-day the circuit printer has broken down—a different fault each time."

"If I were you I would slow down everything else until you

get it right—about ten points should do it."

"Don't look so worried man, we're well ahead of schedule this month. While you're at it, have a look at the records of those two maintenance technicians. That may be your problem. Call me in an hour if you are still in trouble."

He switched off and turned round. "No imagination, these people. We provide them with every sort of aid and yet we still have to do most of their thinking for them. Those machines have automatic fault identification circuits. Correction is nine times out of ten merely a matter of looking it up in the maintenance manual, but those two men didn't seem to know what they were looking for.

"Come on, let's go and have lunch and you can tell me what you've been up to."

Hanson observed his father across the table. He wore his sixty-four years well—no trace of slowing down—just a shade heavier than he used to be perhaps. He was, Hanson thought, a remarkable man in his way. Married to an ambitious and powerful woman and compelled to play second fiddle in his domestic arrangements, he took everything in his stride with the same good-humoured smile. He could have had a brilliant career in the Administrative Service, but marriage had cut that short—a husband in the Service might have been an embarrassment to his wife's political ambitions. Instead he had been given a succession of factories to manage, a sinecure for a man of his talents, not least of which was an ability to get straight to the essentials of a problem. He even got his own way at Board meetings where he was outnumbered three to one by women. The baroness was aware that in many ways his intellect was superior to hers and she occasionally discussed her problems with him. She always listened to what he had to say, even if she did not always follow his advice.

"What brings you back so soon? I thought you were entertaining a Russian friend."

"There is something I want to ask my mother about."

"Anything I can help with?"

Hanson explained about Blanchard but said nothing about Malib. He was not sure yet that there was any connection, though an idea was beginning to form in his mind.

His father sipped his wine thoughtfully. "I'm afraid I can't help you there. I only once remember a matrician being removed from the register. We found out a long time afterwards that he had been executed, but we never did learn what his offence was. These cases do not go through the courts—there is some sort of tribunal that deals with them. I very much doubt if your mother will tell you anything."

He did not have to wait long for the summons. A secretary came through to tell him that the baroness was free and would see him in her office. It was a pity the interview—he always thought of meetings alone with his mother as interviews—was to be held in her office. He felt at a disadvantage there. As a small boy he had never been allowed inside it. Once, when the door had accidentally been left open, he had crept in. He stayed only long enough to catch a glimpse of the desk mounted on a dais at one end of the room. The array of blank monitor screens was somehow menacing and he felt that they were watching him. He rushed straight up to his bedroom where he spent the rest of the day in terror, waiting for the awful retribution that must surely follow such an act of sacrilege. Nothing happened, but the memory of it stayed with him so that, even now, twenty-five years later, he still felt uneasy in it.

She was sitting at her desk now and motioned him to a chair.

"What is it? I have a conference this afternoon and haven't much time to spare."

"It won't take long. I want to know about Tony Blanchard."

Her expression changed from one of impatience to blank

impassivity.

"I was afraid it might be that. He has gone and there is nothing you or anyone else can do about it."

"But why? . . . what has he done? . . . where is he?"

"I'm sorry, I can't discuss it. It is out of my hands." Her hand reached out to the visiphone on her desk as if to signify that the interview was over, then she paused.

"Have you had any thoughts yet about this Malib thing?"

"That was the other thing I wanted to talk about—I want to see the details of the men who were arrested—can that be arranged?"

"Yes—you had better see the judge who dealt with them—I'll get my secretary to arrange it for this afternoon."

She dismissed him with a gesture and he got up to go—the subject of Blanchard was clearly a closed book. Half way to the door he stopped dead in his tracks. How could he have been so stupid? He remembered now the convict on the transit satellite who, Mashenko said, had been staring at him—and the retreating back that had looked vaguely familiar.

He turned round and, keeping his voice quietly casual, said, "Blanchard's on the moon—a convict—isn't he?"

The effect on his mother was electrifying. She became absolutely still, her hand in the air, poised above the visiphone, and there was a menace in her eyes that chilled him to the bone.

"How do you know that? These things are secret—there are no records.

Who told you? I'll . . ."

She did not complete the threat, but let her hand fall slowly to the desk. In all his life he had never before seen her lose her temper. For once she had slipped—he hadn't been certain—only guessing. The temptation to tell her was almost too great to be resisted, but only for a moment—it would not accomplish anything. Instead, he explained the incident on the satellite. This appeared to mollify her and she said, "Since you know that there is no harm in my telling you that he is only there because I commuted his sentence for his mother's sake. He was sentenced to death. That is my last word on the subject."

Two hours later Judge Hilary Cooper, senior Justice of the Metropolitan Bench, leaned back in her chair and contemplated her visitor. That Baroness Alicia Hanson's confidential secretary should have called her was quite flattering. The son, she reflected, was quite someone in his own right too. She couldn't help comparing the man before her with her own husband. Here, she thought, was the sort of man she should have married. With her talents and his family the sky would have been the limit. It was her misfortune to be, if not actually unattractive, certainly nothing to write home about, and because of that she had to put up with a minor bureaucrat in the city administration whose performance in bed was on a par with his career. She was conscious of an unjudicial stirring beneath her magisterial robe.

"When I got Her Excellency's message I sent over to the court for the records you want to see. I also got them to send over one of the videotapes used in evidence. It shows a whole meeting right up to the arrest. Would you like to see that first?"

Hanson, who always made a point of being kind to those who were less well favoured than himself, smiled and said, "It is really extremely kind of you to take so much trouble when you must be so busy. My mother told me that you were the most capable judge on the bench. I see now what she meant."

The judge plugged the recorder into the holoscreen and pointed to a couch in the centre of the room. "You'll be able to see it better from there." She switched on the machine and joined him on the couch.

The film opened with a shot of what appeared to be an untenanted Delta living module – at least there were none of the trappings one would have expected to see in an inhabited flat.

A man came in through the door, a sharp-featured individual wearing a Gamma tunic. He was ill at ease and paced nervously about the room. A little later he was followed by another, also wearing a Gamma tunic. They were obviously strangers to each other. They merely nodded and said nothing. From time to time they glanced covertly at each other and then turned away as if embarrassed. More people began to arrive. There were no greetings, but each newcomer was subjected to a surreptitious scrutiny by the others. The last arrival was a man of middle height wearing a Gamma tunic. He walked with a swagger to the centre of the room and held up his hand.

"My friends," he began, "I bring an apology from the comrade who was to have addressed you to-night. He has been detained by important business and has asked me to talk to you in his stead."

The speaker paused to let this piece of information sink in and then went on in the pompous manner of one who has had unaccustomed glory thrust upon him.

"First of all let me say how happy I am to welcome you to Malib. During the course of this meeting I shall give you an outline of our aims and rules, but, before I begin, there's one rule that I must emphasize right from the start." He paused for effect. "That rule is—Absolute Secrecy. That is the rule that has allowed us to grow from a handful of pioneers to the vast organization we are to-day. Every woman, even your own wife, must be regarded as a potential enemy. If you are summoned to a meeting and cannot come without giving rise to suspicion either at home or at your place of work, then stay away." He emphasized the last two words by thumping his clenched first into the palm of his other hand.

"If you are uncertain whether there is a risk or not, then I must ask you to err on the side of safety. Secrecy and anonymity are our watchwords. I don't know any of you, you don't know me and you don't know each other. You will not see each other until the time comes for us to act. At your next meeting you will see new faces and it will be in a different place."

At this point his audience turned round and looked at one another, not surreptitiously as when they had first come into the room, but openly and boldly. It was as if a weight had been taken off their shoulders.

"We are here, all of us, because for one reason or another we believe that the time has come to end the domination of our society by women. This unnatural state of affairs has lasted for nearly two hundred years—two hundred years too long.

"You must often have asked yourselves why the weaker sex should rule the world. Physically and intellectually we are their superiors—and yet they are our masters. They do not teach you much history in their schools, but there was a time when men ruled the world."

He paused portentously. "How does it come about then that to-day it is the women who rule? It happened, my friends, because our ancestors allowed their heads to be filled with liberal notions about the rights of women. They began by giving married women the power to hold property in their own right; then they gave them political power—allowed them to take part in elections for the country's rulers. All this was done in the name of democracy—yet what did those women do when they finally got power? The first thing they did was to take away from men, and from a great many women too, the right to vote, the right to have a say, however small, in the government of the country."

There was a good deal more of the same sort of stuff. Hanson was unable to gauge the reaction of the audience—their faces were turned away from the camera which was focused on the speaker.

At the end of his harangue the speaker paused and a voice from the back broke in, "That's all very well. What are we going to do about it? What are our plans?"

"Patience my friends, patience. We must have faith in our leader. When the time comes to act you will be told, never fear. Each one of us has been allocated a task and we must make ourselves ready to carry it out when the great day comes. We must keep ourselves fit, mentally and physically so that we can rise and put an end to the power of women. Our movement is growing in strength every day and we are almost ready to act. Remember our watchwords—Secrecy and Anonymity. If our plans were known in advance there would always be the danger of a leak. For your own safety and that of the cause our plans must remain secret right up to the last possible moment."

At that moment the door was broken in and a detachment of police burst into the room. It was over very quickly. Two men rushed at the commander of the detachment and were efficiently clubbed down. The remainder submitted quietly, almost as if they had been expecting it.

Judge Cooper got up and switched the machine off, then returned to her place on the couch.

"Useful that tape—evidence of crime, evidence of arrest, evidence of indentification—all in one. It's not often we get it so neatly packaged. Makes it dull work, of course—all these Malib cases are the same."

"You get many of them then?"

"No, only in the last six months or so—and then only about one a month."

"Are they questioned by the police?"

"Yes, but the answers are always the same—they found a note telling them the time and place of the meeting, and that's all they know.

"What about the speaker? He must know something."

"They know nothing either. The police think they have been programmed over a long period, probably on a hypnopaedic machine—you can apparently do that if you get the right sort of subject. Truth drugs can't penetrate it. They can be de-programmed, of course, but all you get then is a complete blank."

Hanson was silent. He sat back in the couch, chin cupped in his hand, staring into space. Seeing him preoccupied, the judge said, "If you'll excuse me, I'll change out of this robe—I didn't have time before you arrived." She left the room and Hanson was barely aware of her going. There was something nagging at the back of his mind—something to do with the film—that he couldn't pin down.

When she returned she was wearing a loose coat in some sort of flowered material that went strangely with her straight short hair and plain features. The colours were too bright, he decided. Then he remembered the thing that had been puzzling him.

"One thing struck me as odd about that film. Some of these men looked almost as if they had been expecting the police. There was no surprise or alarm on their faces."

"Curious you should say that. The same thought occurred to me when I sentenced them. Usually when a man is sentenced, even if he has known all along what to expect, he shows some sign of distress when he hears the words pronounced, but some of these gave no sign at all."

Hanson was silent again and the judge said, "Can I get you a drink? It helps sometimes." Hanson nodded gratefully. She poured out drinks for both and when she sat down again her coat slipped open exposing a length of not unattractive leg. She made no attempt to adjust it.

"Why are you so interested in Malib—I thought the security people were dealing with it?"

"They don't seem to be able to get anywhere. My mother has asked me to spend some of my leave looking into it—she thinks a man might find a different angle on it."

"What an interesting life you must lead," she smiled,—"not like us poor judges—one dull case after another." As she spoke she moved slightly so that her coat slipped to reveal an expanse of thigh. Hanson made a move to pick up the lists of prisoners. She said, "You needn't bother with those just now—you can take them away and read them at your leisure." She smiled and now there was frank invitation in her eyes.

Afterwards—the judge had proved to be unexpectedly passionate and active—while he was dressing, he discovered that the brief interlude had cleared his mind. He knew what he must do next. He made a quick call on the judge's visiphone and said a hurried good-bye, almost forgetting to take the lists of convicts with him.

Hughes was waiting for him in the outer office. "You caught me just in time. Another few minutes and I should have been gone with the others."

"Can you arrange me a passage back to the moon to-morrow?"

"To-morrow? You are not due to go back for another three and a half weeks. Why the sudden change?"

"Something has cropped up and I must get back as soon as possible."

"Something in connection with the mutual acquaintance we were discussing the other day?"

"In a sense, yes, but not directly."

Hughes permitted his eyebrows to rise a little. "I'll need to check the flight schedule. Let's see if I can work this thing." He went over to the computer terminal on the other side of the room and pressed some keys. When the display flashed on the screen he looked up. "I can fit you in on the ten-thirty shuttle. You are quite sure you want to go?" Hanson nodded and he pressed some more keys.

"What did you discover about our friend—or would that be an indiscreet question?"

"It's just an idea I've had. I may be quite wrong and I'd rather not say anything until I am quite sure." Hughes shrugged his shoulders and said, "You may be fishing in dangerous waters—be careful."

FOUR

When he got back to the flat he noticed that the message-retained lamp on the visiphone was lit up. He flicked a switch and a shame-faced Mashenko appeared on the screen, stammering apologies. "I'm afraid I won't be back until to-night. Leonora has invited me to see her house in the country. I hope it will not inconvenience you." He rushed through the words like a child who has been prompted to recite a party piece. Hanson grinned to himself. That solved one problem—at least he would not have Mashenko on his hands this evening.

He keyed the number of Fiona's flat and after a short delay her face appeared on the screen. She looked anxious.

"What did your mother say?"

"Not much, but I think we had better talk."

"You may take me to dinner. Book a table at Frascati's and I'll meet you there . . . No, on second thoughts—that would mean I should have to get Alaric to escort me—you had better call for me."

That she had chosen Frascati's pleased him. It was one of those expensively discreet places with tables in alcoves, shut off from their neighbours and set at an angle so that you could not see the tables on the other side of the room.

The waiter who led them to their table was wearing a Delta tunic, but, as a concession to a long dead ritual, the tunic was opened part of the way down the front to expose a white shirt surmounted by a black bow. The restaurant itself was a careful blend of ancient and modern. In place of the standard menu books with computer codings for the available dishes there were old-fashioned menu-cards with a comparatively small number of dishes, each one of which was a culinary poem. This was a speciality of Frascati's. Most other restaurants had the standard menu books and a small keyboard on the table on which you ordered your meal in the ordinary way. It was little different from eating at home except that the food was brought to you by a waiter when it arrived at the service hatch. At Frascati's, if you were bold enough, you could order slight variations on the dishes on the menu and, because of this, they were able to charge nearly twice as much as any other restaurant in London.

Fiona ordered drinks and they sat sipping them while they studied the menu. Without consulting him she chose a simple but exquisitely concocted meal of the sort that Frascati's excelled at, and a modest but entirely suitable wine. By unspoken consent they made no mention of Blanchard, but kept their conversation on a purely personal level. For once Hanson was grateful for the matrician convention that one never discussed business or other serious matters during a meal.

Fiona drew him like a magnet until he found that he was talking about himself as he had never done before. She, too, let herself be drawn and they lost themselves in the sheer delight of discovering each other. The exquisite meal slipped down almost without their being aware of it. It was only when the waiter had brought their coffee and retired discreetly after dimming the lights that they emerged reluctantly from the cocoon which they had woven about themselves.

It was Fiona who broke the spell, leaning forward, a troubled look in her dark eyes. "What did your mother say?"

Hanson hesitated—he had not been looking forward to this moment.

"This is going to be a shock to you, I'm afraid. Blanchard is a convict on the moon."

"Oh no," she whispered, "not that. It can't be—there must be some mistake. They don't do that to matricians.

What is he supposed to have done?"

"I don't know yet," he said softly. "She refused point blank to say any more—but I'll find out."

He leaned forward and put his hand over hers—it was the first time he had touched her. He said, with a confidence he did not feel, "Don't worry, I think I may be able to do something about it—I have booked a passage to the moon to-morrow."

"Do you think that was what he meant when he said that the moon was the key?"

He shook his head, "I don't think so. From what my mother said he couldn't have known he would be sent there." He had decided to say nothing about the death sentence. "That is something I don't quite understand yet."

They were still sitting like that, Hanson's hand over Fiona's when a voice broke in, "Well this is a surprise. What a small world it is." Hanson withdrew his hand and looked up. It was Lumsden, dressed in the mess uniform of the Guards and contemplating them with a smile which had no counterpart in his eyes.

Fiona spoke first. "Alaric! What are you doing here? Have you been following me?" There was a sharpness in her voice that Hanson had not heard before.

"As a matter of fact, I was at a loose end this evening and I looked in here to see if there was anyone I knew, but I see that you have no need of other company."

Fiona bridled. "Not at all. Would you care to join us for a drink? We were just about to order some brandy."

Lumsden glanced at his watch and said, "Thank you, but I have left it too late. I'm due in the mess shortly for a game of cards. Some other time perhaps."

He clicked his heels and bowed. When he had gone, Fiona said, "I'm getting bored with Alaric—he's becoming tiresome. I almost think he is jealous."

She grinned conspiratorially across the table. Hanson flushed with pleasure and, because he could think of nothing appropriate to say, he held up a hand to summon a waiter and order brandy.

Lumsden's interruption seemed to have brought them closer together. They were content to sip their brandy in silence and look into each other's eyes from time to time. Fiona's hand slid across the table towards him and he placed his own over it again.

At last, after what seemed a long time, Fiona withdrew her hand gently and said, "If you are going to the moon to-morrow, you must have things to do. Perhaps you had better take me home now."

They scarcely spoke until he put the heliplane down on the roof of Fiona's block of flats. As they landed a burly guard emerged from her shelter beside the lift shaft and stood watching them as they crossed the roof, her hand on the butt of her stun-ray. She saluted when she recognized Fiona, but continued to keep an eye on them. Fiona whispered, "Good-bye, be careful," squeezed his hand impulsively and then was gone.

He allowed the plane to drift back gently towards Richmond with the rotor turning and the jets barely wafting it along. He was still bemused as he walked towards the lift shaft and did not notice a movement behind one of the ventilators. There was a faint plop behind him and he felt a sharp stabbing pain in the back of his neck. Then the darkness descended on him.

He came round slowly, dragging himself up from immense depths. His first sensation was of cold, a damp clammy cold that enveloped his whole body. Gradually he became aware of other sensations. He was lying on something hard and uneven that was digging into his shoulder. There was something else, something he could not identify at first, familiar but somehow out of place. It was a breeze—but it couldn't be, and he drifted down again, just below the level of consciousness. He tried to stay there but the cold reached into his bones and he stirred. He shivered and curled up his body to shut it out. Then he became aware of a new sensation—his hand had touched something wet. With a superhuman effort he forced his eyes open, then shut them quickly against the dazzling brightness. He struggled to open them again and saw that what had dazzled him was the sun. Then he sat up, wide awake.

He was in a clearing on a low hillside with trees on either side of him. The sun had just risen above the tree-tops on the other side of the valley and, in the distance was a river, only partly visible through the trees and undergrowth. He looked at his watch and saw that it was a little after six. Then it all came back to him—the evening with Fiona and the sharp pain in the back of his neck before he had passed out. He put his hand up and felt his neck. There was a small swelling, still painful to the touch. It must have been a tranquillizer dart, but a powerful one. Mostly their effect lasted only for an hour or so. This one must have been intended for a large animal. He had been lucky—he remembered hearing somewhere of a zoo attendant who had been accidentally killed by a dart intended for a rhinoceros. He shivered, not entirely from the cold, and dragged himself to his feet. Someone wanted him out of the way—but who and why?

There was no answer he could think of. That question would have to wait. The first thing to do was to find out where he was. To the north, still hazy in the early morning sunshine, the ground appeared to rise steeply. To the west and east there was lower ground with undulating hills. The horizon was lost in the mist. His arms and legs were stiff from the night's exposure and he climbed painfully to the top of the small rise on which he was standing. When he got there he saw that, to the south, there was nothing but forest that stretched as far as the eye could see.

He sat down to take stock. The faint warmth from the early morning sun was beginning to penetrate the dampness of his clothing. He went through his pockets and found that nothing seemed to be missing. Even his identity card had been left. Whoever kidnapped him must have been in a hurry. He put his hand down and felt for the small laser. It was still there. He studied the countryside again, trying to find something in the landscape he could identify. He wished now that he had learned more about local geography. All the same, there was something vaguely familiar in the lie of the land. He scanned it slowly, then closed his eyes and, after a moment, opened them again. He was in the Game Park and somewhere to the south must be the Collection Centre he had seen the other day on his visit with Mashenko.

Mashenko—he wondered if he had returned to the flat yet. Perhaps Leonora had persuaded him to spend another night with her. How long would it be before someone realized that he had disappeared? Even if Mashenko had gone back to the flat last night it might be several hours before he asked any questions. Hughes would be told about his failure to report for his flight to the moon, but would he do anything about it? There was no reason why he should. People must fail to turn up for their flights from time to time for all sorts of perfectly ordinary reasons. Anyway, it was a futile speculation—nobody would have any idea where to start looking for him. There was nothing for it but to begin walking due south. That way, even if he missed the Collection Centre, he would be bound to come to the hunting area which he knew well from his schooldays.

This would be a very different sort of expedition. He surveyed his equipment ruefully—the laser in his trouser fly and a pocket-knife too small to be of any use as a weapon. Both these were considered by his friends to be mild eccentricities and they chaffed him about them from time to time. The laser was simply a cutting tool. Most of his life he had suffered slightly from claustrophobia and he had a horror of being shut in a closed compartment if the electronic lock failed, as they sometimes did. The laser was powerful enough to cut through most materials, but he doubted its effectiveness as a weapon except at close range. The pocket-knife was a legacy from his schooldays. Old

Gregg, the school huntsman, had got him into the habit. He used to say, "You can have all the weapons and modern gimmicks you like, but you never know when your life might depend on a good old-fashioned knife." It looked as if he might have been right, after all. He took off his tunic and turned it outside in. The scarlet and blue badge of his class would be altogether too conspicuous in these surroundings where the condition of survival was to see without being seen.

The going was tougher than he had expected. The trees for the most part were well spaced but there was a thick tangle of brambles and ground-ivy which slowed him down. After four hours he judged that he had not covered more than nine or ten miles. His hands and legs were scratched and bleeding and he was hungry. It was long past breakfast time and so far all he had eaten was a handful of wild strawberries which were not quite ripe. He gritted his teeth and pushed on. After a little the going became easier with large clearings here and there through which he made better time. This part of the park appeared to have been deserted. He had not come across any signs of people having passed that way, nor had he seen much in the way of game—only a solitary rabbit and, once, some young pheasants running on ahead of him until they disappeared through a gap in the bushes.

By midday he calculated that he had come about fourteen miles from his starting point and he lay down to rest at the edge of a clearing. The sun was hot now and he dozed off. When he opened his eyes the first thing he saw was a rabbit about twenty yards away at the edge of the trees. He lay perfectly still and watched it. Slowly it came nearer, stopping to nibble at the grass, then hopping a yard or two towards him. Very carefully, an inch at a time he moved his hand towards his trouser fly, then stopped. He remembered that he had transferred the laser to his trouser pocket before he started walking. It was in his right-hand pocket and he was lying on it.

Gently he began to raise his right thigh off the ground.

The rabbit stopped nibbling and sat perfectly still, its head slightly raised and alert. Hanson froze and held his breath. If he were to move now it would be off. The strain on his ankle was almost unbearable. The rabbit took a few hops towards him and began to nibble. Hanson took a deep breath and continued edging his thigh upwards until he could slip his fingers inside the pocket and grasp the end of the laser. Inch by inch he began to withdraw it, still supported on his ankle. The rabbit was still nibbling and inching towards him.

Now came the difficult part—he had to get his arm out from under his body and raise it to shoulder level before it would bear on the rabbit which was in range now, but only just. Carefully he moved his forearm from under him until his elbow was clear. He relaxed a moment, then continued moving his arm through the grass, scarcely daring to breathe. The rabbit stopped nibbling and raised its head, snuffling suspiciously. It was now or never. He sat up quickly, pushing the switch forward, and a pencil of blue light hit the ground in front of the rabbit which froze into rigidity. He moved his hand a fraction and the beam caught it full in the head. There was a faint sizzling sound and the rabbit keeled over. The laser had cut a neat hole straight through its head. The knowledge that he now had some food revived him and he decided to push on, stopping only to gut the rabbit which he tied to a loop on his trousers with some twisted strands of grass.

In the late afternoon he began to find traces of human activity. There were distinct paths through the trees and, at the edge of a clearing, he came across the insides of a large animal, probably a deer. To judge from the flies, they had not been there more than a day or two. He moved more warily now, his ears alert for the slightest sound. At every clearing he stopped and searched carefully for any sign of life before crossing it. The country was changing now. The clearings were more frequent and from time to time he came across tumbled heaps of stones which had once been farm buildings.

Towards evening he came to the remains of what must once have been a large house. The walls were completely overgrown, so much so that he almost missed it. The surrounding trees and undergrowth had evidently protected it from the worst ravages of wind and weather and the walls were almost intact up to seven or eight feet. A small weed-choked stream, not much more than a ditch, ran past one end of it. He went inside. Only the outside walls remained standing and there was nothing to show where the inside walls had been. Someone had built a primitive fireplace in the centre of the building and there were a few bones scattered about. The stones were well blackened and showed signs of having been used more than once, but there was no trace of ashes. It looked as if it had not been used for some time. He decided to take a chance and camp here for the night.

He skinned the rabbit and cooked it whole over a fire of dead wood. It was a slow process and the result was not attractive—charred on the outside and not quite enough cooked on the inside. He gnawed it ravenously, saving only the two hind legs, and washed it down with water scooped up from the stream. Then he wrapped the hind legs in dock leaves and tucked them inside his tunic.

Afterwards he used the laser to cut down some branches and built himself a lean-to shelter which would at least serve to keep the dew off him. The last thing he did before going to sleep was to transfer the laser from his pocket to the pouch on his trouser fly.

He did not know at first what had wakened him, only that he was suddenly wide awake and alert. He lay quite still, listening. A man's voice in the distance called out something unintelligible and an answering shout came from further away. Hanson eased himself out of his improvised shelter and moved cautiously into the bushes. From what he had heard of the Game Park it would be prudent to treat every man as a potential enemy in the absence of evidence to the contrary.

There was another shout and this time he was able to gauge its direction roughly. It seemed to be coming from a large clearing he had noticed on his approach to the ruin. He moved slowly towards it, conscious that every sound he made would be magnified in the stillness of the night. When he got near to the clearing he lay down and wriggled the last few yards. In the moonlight he could make out a red glow surrounded by several indistinct figures. The glow suddenly burst into flame and the figures moved back from it. One of them pointed skywards. At first Hanson could see nothing, then he heard the characteristic fripping of a heliplane's rotor. The machine landed and the figures clustered round it.

He saw nothing more until the plane took off again. Then the figures in the clearing began moving in his direction and he realized that he was in a direct line between them and the ruined farmhouse. He got up and ran, stumbling through the undergrowth until he was well clear of their line. As they came level with them he could hear them talking to one another but could not make out what they were saying. He raised his head cautiously and peered through the bushes. Three men were struggling through the undergrowth with a large box which appeared to be heavy. He heard one of them curse as he tripped over a branch.

Hanson waited five minutes and cautiously made his way back towards the ruin. He edged his way towards the wall that was in shadow. He could hear the voices clearly now. They were arguing. A nervous, rather high-pitched voice was saying, "I don't care what you say, someone's been here to-night. This shelter wasn't here yesterday and that rabbit carcase is fresh. I tell you I don't like it."

Another voice chipped in, "Stop bleating for Christ's sake, Gage. It was probably a convict stopping off for the night. There are a few round about—I saw one myself yesterday."

Another voice, more educated this time, broke in, "Shut up, both of you. Somebody has been here to-night and gone again. Why would he go to the bother of building a shelter and then clear off? He must have heard us. I think we had better take a look outside. Jack, you and Barney take a torch. You had better take one of these as well." There was a sound of metal knocking against metal.

Hanson quickly took stock of his position. He was trapped—no chance of getting away. There was a tangle of brambles a couple of yards away. That would have to do. He wriggled painfully into it and, for once, did not feel the thorns scratching his hands and face. He curled up into a ball and buried his face in the ground so that there would be no tell-tale reflection in the moonlight. Footsteps came towards him and he froze.

"Don't waste time looking there. If there was anyone, he's well away from the house by now. How the hell does Baker expect us to find anything in this lot? You'd need a whole bloody army to search it. It's all a waste of time if you ask me. Come on, let's go down towards the clearing. That's the only place we're likely to see anything."

The footsteps moved away and Hanson breathed again. A trickle of blood from a scratch on his forehead went into his eye and he twisted his arm free to wipe it away, then ducked again. A man had come round the corner of the ruin and was making in his direction. The footsteps approached, then stopped. The man stamped about as if trampling something. Then there was silence followed by a rustling sound. Hanson slowly raised his head and opened his eyes. Not two yards from where he lay a man was squatting with his trousers pulled down. He moved his head to relieve a crick in his neck and a thorn stabbed his eye. He couldn't help the automatic reaction. His head jerked back and he clapped a hand over his eye.

"——! Baker, Charlie, there's some bastard here—quick."

There was a sound of running feet and two pairs of hands

dragged him out from the brambles. He was pulled roughly to his feet and one of his captors brought his clenched fist down sideways across his face, almost knocking him down.

"What the bleeding hell were you doing, hiding in there?"

The educated voice which he had heard before called out, "Lay off, you bloody fool. Take him inside and let's have a look at him."

He was pushed inside the ruin and a torch turned full on his face. The educated voice said, "Suppose you tell me what you were doing out there."

Hanson looked coldly at him and said nothing.

"I asked you a question. Do you want me to beat it out of you?" He raised a clenched fist threateningly. Hanson said coldly, "I could ask you the same question."

A man exclaimed, "— —! A bleeding matrician. What's he doing here?"

"Shut up Hogan. Leave this to me."

He turned to Hanson again, "So, a matrician, eh? Now you will have to do some explaining and it had better be good." He reached forward and pulled up Hanson's sleeve. "No number tattooed there, so you're not a convict—not that they would send one of your kind here, no matter what you had done. Come on, out with it." He brought his first hard across Hanson's face. There was no mistaking the hostility now.

"I was kidnapped and dumped in the Park about twenty miles north of here.
I was making my way south and decided to camp here for the night. You woke me up and, naturally, I got out of the way until I knew whether it was safe to show myself.

"Kidnapped—I don't believe it. You'll have to do better than that."

One of the men holding him began to twist his arm up behind his back. Hanson said through clenched teeth, "If you don't believe me, look at the back of my neck and you'll see a puncture made by a tranquillizer dart."

His questioner examined the puncture and nodded.

"That looks like a tranquillizer all right, and a big one at that. You're lucky to be alive."

"I think someone wanted to kill me."

"In that case, why put you down in the park?"

"It's not so easy to dispose of a body in London."

"If they thought you were dead, why bother to put you down gently? Why not simply drop you from a height?"

"The passenger seats in a heliplane are behind the pilot. He would have to get out before he could dump me."

"That sounds reasonable. Have you been lying where we found you since we woke you up?"

"Yes—I'd only just got there when you arrived." There was no point in letting them know that he had seen the heliplane.

The man scratched his chin thoughtfully. "Well, no harm done, but you can't stay here. Let him go." The two men who had been holding his arms released him and the man said, "You two go with him and make sure he gets well away from here."

Hanson breathed an almost audible sigh of relief and moved towards the entrance, but it proved to be premature. The two men who had been sent to search the area chose that moment to return. They stared at Hanson.

"Where did you find him?"

"Where you ought to have done if you'd been doing your job properly. A bloody fine search party you are. God knows who chose you for this." The smaller of the two searchers bridled. "Sod you, Baker, we didn't choose you for a boss either. We'd have made a better job of it if we had. Anyway, we did find something. The grass by the clearing was all flattened—someone had been lying there. We found signs of a track leading back this way."

The man called Baker swung round to Hanson. "You lied—you did see something then." Before Hanson could reply he was seized again.

"Let's kill the bastard. We can't take any chances. His kind are for the chop anyway—might as well do it now."

Baker whirled on the speaker. "You never learn, do you Charlie. If he's been sent here we want to find out who sent him and why. He'll have to be kept here till to-morrow night's drop and sent back for questioning. They'll know how to make him talk."

He turned to the man called Charlie. "You and Barney are waiting here for the drop. You'll have to keep an eye on him as well. Keep that gun and use it if you have to. If you so much as let him out of your sight for half a second, I'll kill you. You'll have to take it in turns to sleep."

He turned to the others. "The rest of us better get moving. We've wasted enough time as it is—it will be daylight in a couple of hours."

He went over to the large box which was lying in the centre of the floor. "Come on, take four of these each and get moving."

When they had gone, the man called Barney swaggered over to Hanson and brandished a stun-ray at him. "See this, mate. One move out of you and I'll let you have it." He aimed the gun at him. "I've a good mind to do it anyway—save us the trouble of staying awake."

"For ——sake, Barney, you heard what Baker said—use it if you have to. Baker's got his knife into you already. Give him half a chance an' he'll finish you off."

"All right then, sod you, but you can take the first spell—I'm going to get some sleep." He handed the gun over to the man called Charlie and composed himself to sleep in the shelter which Hanson had built. Charlie brandished the gun at Hanson and said, "Don't you get any ideas, mate. I'll let you have it as soon as look at you."

Hanson glanced coldly at him, shrugged his shoulders and sat down in the corner with his back against the wall. He made himself as comfortable as was possible in the circumstances and sat calmly gazing at Charlie, no trace of expression on his face. This went on for several minutes. Charlie, disconcerted by the steady, unwavering stare, began to fidget, shifting his feet uneasily. He affected an interest in his stun-ray. Hanson guessed that he had never had one in his hands before. He turned it over, fiddled with the safety catch, took aim at a stone and pulled the trigger. Nothing happened. Worried, he fiddled with the safety catch some more and pulled the trigger again. Still nothing happened. He grinned uneasily at Hanson, "Just practising," then went and sat on a stone facing him with the gun cradled in his lap. They sat like that for a long time, neither saying anything. When the sound of snoring from the shelter told him that Barney was asleep Hanson stood up and walked over to the other corner, unzipping his fly on the way. Charlie jumped to his feet. "Hey you can't do that here—we gotta live in this."

Hanson shrugged and walked over to the exit. Charlie, clutching the gun followed close behind him, suspicious and alert. Once outside he walked along the wall away from the entrance until Charlie called out, "That'll do." Modestly, he turned his back to Charlie and slipped the laser from its pouch. When he had finished he continued to stand on the same spot. Charlie came up behind him and prodded him with the gun. "Come on, what are you waiting for? Back inside." Hanson turned round, still zipping up his fly and switched on the laser. The beam caught Charlie in the foot and he screamed in agony, dropping the gun.

Hanson picked it up and dashed into the building. Barney, awakened by the scream, was pulling himself out from the shelter. Hanson fired the stun-ray and he collapsed in a heap on the floor. He returned to Charlie who by this time had taken off his boot and was rocking to and fro in agony, clutching his foot. Hanson grasped the neck of his tunic and dragged him inside. There were tears in the little man's eyes. "You bastard," he spat out. "What have you done to him?"

"He's only stunned—he'll come round in a few hours."

"You've burnt a hole through my bloody foot, you bastard," Charlie moaned, still writhing about on the ground.

"I'm going to burn some more holes in you in a minute unless you talk—I want to know what is going on here."

"Go to hell."

Hanson pointed the laser at the ground in front of the little man's feet and switched it on. Some dried twigs burst into flame and disappeared in smoke. Charlie screamed, "No, no. I'll tell you, I'll tell you."

Hanson switched off the beam. "Good, we'll start with the stun-rays. Where did they come from and what are they for?"

"I don't know where they came from—honest I don't—only from the heliplane."

"And what are they to be used for?"

Charlie hesitated and Hanson carefully aimed the laser at him. "Come on, it will be a bigger hole this time."

"I don't know, I don't know." His voice rose to a scream. "All I know is we got to collect together with the others and wait for orders to attack."

"Attack what?"

"I don't know, I swear I don't . . . something about some houses . . . matrician houses, I think."

"Where are you meeting the others?"

"I can't tell you exactly, Guv, but I know how to get there. It's a big place, about two hours south of here, with a sort of roof of branches on it."

"How many of you are there?"

"A dozen . . . twenty maybe. I'm not sure—I haven't seen them all. They don't tell us much—only what we need to know."

"Who are they?"

"Malib—Organization for Male Liberation—that's us. We're gonna kill your lot—and your bloody women too." He spat at Hanson but missed.

"Twenty of you? I don't believe that." Hanson raised the laser again. This time he switched it on and the pencil of intense blue light struck the ground about a yard from

Charlie, then moved slowly towards him leaving a smoking black trail behind it.

"All right, all right, I'll tell you, you bastard," he screamed. "We're not the main attack—that's somewhere else. They haven't told us." He suddenly became defiant again. "You can knock us all out in the park—but that won't stop us. You lot have had it."

Clearly there was nothing more to be learned from this source. Hanson slipped the laser into his pocket and picked up the stun-ray. The little man looked up at him fearfully. "What are you going to do now?"

"I'm sending you to join Barney. When you come round you had better get well away from here. Your friends won't be too pleased when they find I have gone."

Charlie opened his mouth to protest, but no sound came from him as the stun-ray found its mark.

Hanson wasted no time getting out of the place. Thanks to his late captors he was better equipped than when he had started out. The stun-ray had an effective range of about thirty yards and would be more useful for getting game than the laser—not that he expected to need it for that. He had found some cold meat in the box that had held the weapons—it looked like venison—and he had left behind the two rabbit legs which he thought were a fair exchange in the circumstances.

There was a faint glow of promised daylight in the eastern sky as he set out. It was in fact a beautiful morning. The trees still had that air of mystery which the darkness gives them and, from time to time, a bird tried out the first few notes of its morning song.

Now that he was effectively armed there was no need to keep to the trees and he made use of the clearings and open ground, even if it meant a detour. Time had suddenly become more important. At most he had twenty-four hours before the Malib group came looking for him. This time they would not make any mistakes. He had signed his death warrant as far as they were concerned. There was another thing. Once the Malib organizers, whoever they were, learned that he had escaped with knowledge of their activities in the park, they might be forced to put their plan into action before he could get back to civilization. Otherwise they would have to abandon it completely. Luckily he had turned in early and had all the sleep he would need for the next twenty hours or so. He walked quickly now, but with all his senses alert—he did not want to run into Baker and his gang.

After he had been walking for about three hours he came to a small stream. He stopped there and ate some of the venison. By now the sun was fully up in the sky and the early morning mist had cleared except for a thick blanket still clinging to the valley in front of him. After a brief rest he pushed on into the mist which still persisted. It was not long before he found out why—there was a river blocking his path. It was about a hundred yards wide and the bank on his side was marshy. No doubt it was the same on the other side. He took off his shoes and squelched his way to the bank proper. As far as he could see, neither upstream nor down was there any broken water which might indicate shallows or a ford. He had no way of telling how deep it was. He stripped naked, rolling up the gun and his clothes in his tunic which he managed to secure round his neck with the closure band. The water was cold but refreshing. He had not realized how badly he needed a bath.

He was half way across when he saw the heliplane, flying low and coming straight towards him through the mist. He trod water and waved and shouted, but it was no use. Either the pilot did not see him or was not interested. The mist was still draped across the water and he might well not be visible, but it was clear enough for Hanson to see that it was one of the regular patrol planes.

He wondered how often they patrolled. It might be days before one crossed his path again. His chance of being picked up by one was beginning to look rather slim.

As he had guessed, the other bank was just as marshy as

the one he had left and he had to go some distance before reaching firm ground. He did not stop to dress himself but made straight for some trees a hundred yards away. His nakedness made the open ground seem dangerously exposed and he walked quickly, heedless of the damage he was doing to his feet.

It was pleasant lying naked in the morning sunshine and he felt clean for the first time since waking up in the park. Reluctantly he dressed himself and started off southwards. By now he must be well past the spot where Baker and the others had taken the weapons. There was no more danger from that quarter.

There were, however, other dangers. When he had gone about another mile he came to a large clearing and decided to cut straight across it. He had reached the middle when he noticed the dark shapes at the far edge. They were difficult to identify against the background of the trees. After he had gone about another hundred yards he realized that they were a herd of wild cattle, fairly harmless beasts as he remembered. The bull thought otherwise and came charging out as if he thought that Hanson was about to usurp the affections of his cows. The great shaggy beast tore across the ground at a speed which left him no chance to make the safety of the trees. There was no time to get the laser out from its pouch. He slipped off the safety catch of the stun-ray. It no longer gave him confidence—it was after all designed to work on the human brain. A massive bull weighing half a ton was a different proposition. This, unfortunately was one of the standard issue guns with no provision for increasing the power. He waited until the bull was about twenty yards away, head lowered and the wicked-looking horns aimed at his belly, then squeezed the trigger and held it that way. At first it made no difference and the animal kept coming. Then, only a few yards from him, its head hit the ground and the huge body somersaulted. Hanson jumped out of the way as the momentum of the charge carried it past him. He did not stop to examine it, but made his way quickly across the clearing, giving the cows a wide berth, an unnecessary precaution as it turned out. Unmoved by the fate of their lord and master, they stood grouped together, following him only with their eyes.

Hanson was not superstitious but he recalled a saying that good luck—and bad—came in threes. The river and the bull made two. He wondered what the third might be. An hour later he found it in the shape of a thick forest which stretched on either side as far as the eye could see. There was nothing for it but to go straight through it and hope for the best.

Three hours later he stumbled out into open country, his clothes torn and his hands bleeding from a hundred scratches. He emerged at the top of a small hill and saw before him the hilly ground and rocky outcrops that characterized the country round the collection centre. Below him on the right was an almost dried-up watercourse which wound its way round the side of the hill. He clambered down to it and found a small pool set between two great limestone boulders and fed by a tiny trickle of water from above. Kneeling down beside it, he scooped up handful after handful of the brackish water, bathed his hands in it, then took off his shoes and did the same for his feet.

There was enough of the venison left to provide him with two more meals if he was careful. He ate half of it and lay down for a short rest. His long sojourn on the moon had not been the best preparation for this sort of test. He ached in every limb and his hands were beginning to stiffen from the cuts and scratches, as also were his knees. Exhaustion overcame him and he struggled in vain to keep his eyes open.

When he woke up he was cold and shivering in spite of the warmth of the evening sun. He looked at his watch and started to his feet—he had been asleep for almost two hours. He jumped up and down to dispel the chill and loosen up his legs which were stiffer now than when he had lain down. There were still a few hours of daylight left before he would have to stop for the night. It was unlikely that he would be picked up now—it might be days before another patrol came his way.

As it happened, he was wrong, but he almost missed it. The going was difficult, rough grass and limestone outcrops, so that he had to keep his eyes on the ground to avoid tripping over the stones that lay in his path. Had he not glanced up to check his bearings he might have missed altogether the brief flash of sunlight reflected from the heliplane's transparent canopy. It was travelling on a course that would take it a few hundred yards to his right. He took off his tunic and waved it frantically. There was just a chance that the scarlet and blue material would be bright enough to catch the pilot's eye. When the plane was almost level with him he redoubled his efforts and shouted but it continued on its way northwards. Then it swung round in a wide circle and came slowly towards him. He could see that the pilot had started up the rotor. It came nearer until he could make out the pilot's head through the canopy. Slowly it circled him, maintaining its height, and it dawned on Hanson that the pilot might not bother to land. A convict waving to a passing patrol might well be a common accurrence. He sought for some way to convince her that he was not an ordinary inhabitant of the park. Hurriedly he pulled the laser from his pockets, turned it up to full power and aimed it at a gorse bush about five yards away. The narrow pencil of vivid blue light hit the bush and a branch turned to white heat. Seconds later the bush was a mass of flames.

The response was instantaneous. A woman's voice issued from a loudspeaker.

"Throw away that laser or I'll blast you off the face of the earth."

He did so and the plane came down to land about ten yards away. The hatch slid open followed by a woman in the uniform of the park patrol.

"I've got this gun on full power. It can kill you. Put your hands over your head and walk slowly towards me."

Hanson did as he was told. There was something vaguely familiar about the pilot. As he came up with her he recognized her—it was the same girl who had taken him over the park with Mashenko. "What the devil was her name?

"Ah, Miss Wilson—am I glad to see you."

She peered at him suspiciously. Two days' growth of beard and a mass of scratches had changed his appearance somewhat. "How do you know my name?"

"The day before yesterday you took me round the park with a Russian friend."

The stun-ray wavered a little, then dropped. "It's . . . it's Mr Hanson, isn't it? But how . . ."

"Let me pick up my things and I'll explain."

Seated in the plane he said, "Before we start, call your warden and ask her to let my mother know I am here and to send a plane to fetch me." He gave her his mother's private number.

On the way back he gave the girl a brief account of what had happened, omitting any reference to the Malib contingent. That, he thought, he had better keep to himself for the time being.

The warden herself was waiting for him on the roof, a study in suppressed curiosity, and led him to her office.

"Her Excellency's plane is on its way. Is there anything I can do for you till it arrives?"

Hanson shook his head, "There is only one thing—I don't want my kidnappers to know I have escaped. Will you make sure that nothing gets out. I suppose you can trust the officer who brought me in?"

"You need have no fear about that—she won't talk—she is one of our best officers."

"Better send for her. I owe it to her to tell her myself."

When she came in he said, "First of all I want to thank

you. If it hadn't been for you I might have been there for days—might never have got out at all, in fact."

"There is no need to thank me. I thought at first you were a convict who had gone round the bend—we get them sometimes. I would have left you there if it had not been for the laser. That was enough to tell me you were not a convict." She paused. "You know, if you had not put it down when I asked I would have killed you."

"I'm very glad you didn't. There is one thing more—who knows you brought me back?"

"Only the warden, sir."

"Good. I'd be glad if you keep it that way."

He turned to the warden. "When you called my mother did you speak to anyone else?"

"No, the baroness herself answered the visiphone. She's a cool one, if you'll forgive me—didn't ask any questions, just said, 'Very well, I'll send a plane for him', and then rang off."

"Tell me, do you patrol the park after dark?"

"No, that would mean doubling our staff and, as you know, the whole point of the Game Park is that it provides maximum prison accommodation at minimum cost—no expensive buildings to be maintained, no large staff of warders and, of course, no prisoners' meals to be found. Our total staff, apart from my deputy, is six officers—not even a clerk. We lose a few prisoners, of course. Some don't survive and some prefer to stay on—there must be several hundred there by now."

Hanson nodded. That explained why his kidnapper had been able to dump him in the park. It also explained the night heliplane landings. It would be possible to assemble a small army in the park without being discovered.

The arrival of the baroness's private heliplane put an end to the conversation. Ten minutes later Hanson climbed out on to the landing-pad at his mother's house.

An hour later, bathed, shaved and fed, and free from all

cuts and scratches, thanks to a liberal application of tissue-restoring cream, he sat facing the baroness in her private sitting-room. She was taking it very calmly, even for her. There had been no expressions of surprise or relief and no questions. All she said was, "Come to my sitting-room when you have cleaned up and eaten."

She listened without interruption to his account of what had happened and, when he had finished, said, "So much for that. Now suppose you tell me what it means."

"I think that Malib are planning a coup and that it isn't very far away."

"A coup—with a handful of convicts in the Game Park? Don't be ridiculous."

Hanson hesitated. The idea was so fantastic that he himself could scarcely believe it, but there was no other interpretation that made any sense at all. He wished that his evidence was less tenuous.

"The main attack that man mentioned . . . it can only be . . . the moon." His mother said nothing but sat contemplating him as if she were looking for some further evidence of insanity. Then she said quietly, "Go on."

"Suppose you were a revolutionary and wanted to overthrow the World Government, how would you go about it?"

She considered this for a little and said, "I don't think it would be possible. No country has more weapons than are needed for internal policing and they are strictly controlled. All the potential revolutionaries are walled up in the cities with no means of escape. Anyway, assassinating a handful of people at the top would not be enough. You would have to kill thousands of people scattered all over the world. It can't be done—the whole idea is absurd."

The scarcely concealed contempt in her tone stung Hanson to reply, "You women are so damned complacent. You don't have to kill off people to overpower a government. There is a more effective way—you simply make it impossible for it to govern."

"I don't see what this has to do with the moon." Her tone was icy cold.

"Your predecessors were obsessed withthe idea of making wars impossible and they succeeded, but in the process they constructed a machine that could be used to destroy the world. They concentrated everything on the moon and put it under international control." The baroness interrupted, "Do you mean nuclear reactors? Are you suggesting that Malib plan to capture the moon and make nuclear weapons?"

Hanson shook his head. "Perhaps you have forgotten the satellite power stations that supply all our electricity. When they were built provision was made for them to be switched off in an emergency. So far there has never been an emergency, but the equipment is still there—on the moon. Like every other vital system on the moon, it has four separate keys, all of which must be operated before it can be brought into use. One key is held by the senior commissioner from each national group."

"I know all that. Why don't you come to the point?"

"The point, dear mother, is that twenty people, five from each group, and totally without defence of any kind, control the whole operation. Capture them and you can virtually control the world."

The baroness was visibly shaken. She had clearly not considered this possibility.

"But how could they get there in the first place?"

"I have an idea about that, but I can't be sure yet. I left some papers in my flat. If you can arrange for them to be picked up, they may give us the answer."

The baroness left the room to give the necessary instructions—her sitting-room was strictly for relaxing in and did not boast even a visiphone extension. There was only a bell push for the domestic staff.

When she returned her voice had lost some of its edge and she offered him a drink. "Your Russian friend is coming here to-morrow—the poor man has been worried about you.

So, apparently, has Mary Hamilton's daughter."

"How did she know? As far as she was concerned I was on my way back to the moon."

"Hughes from Space Transport called your flat when you failed to show up for your flight. When he got no reply he rang her and then, since she knew nothing, he called me. By the way, why were you going to the moon?"

He debated whether to tell her about Blanchard's cryptic message but decide to keep it to himself for the time being. There was still something he didn't understand about that. Instead he said, "I had an idea that I might learn something there—it seems now as if I was right." The baroness said nothing. She was clearly not convinced yet.

Later, as they said good-night, she said, "By the way, I asked that girl down to-morrow when I knew you were back." She was her old self again. Fiona was going to be vetted. The fact that there was as yet no reason for it would not deter her. It was part of her creed to be one step ahead of any situation that might crop up.

He tumbled into bed and slept like the dead.

It was nine o'clock before he came down to breakfast and found his mother waiting for him. She had not been idle. On the table in front of her was a pile of computer print-outs. She said, "It is beginning to look as if you were right. The information you had in your flat only went back six months. I've gone back another twelve months. There hasn't been a change in the pattern of convictions—they began to increase about seven months ago. Not by many—two or three a month. The interesting thing is that they were all Gammas who do not usually run foul of the law. There are now two computer programmers doing time on the moon, four mining machinery technicians, three laboratory assistants and, curiously, twelve professional footballers. There have also been a few Gammas sent to the Game Park."

Hanson was excited now, but forced himself to maintain

an almost casual air. "I'm sure now that I was right—the footballers clinch it." His mother gave him a puzzled stare. "Footballers?"

"Yes, the nearest thing to true fighting men left on the earth. Each one of them knows more ways of crippling a man than all your police put together—and they practise it every day. Even unarmed they would be more than a match for the prison warders on the moon."

He got up from the table and paced the room. "We must do something quickly. By now the group in the Game Park will have discovered my escape and alerted their leaders, whoever they are. It may force them to move sooner than they had intended."

"If you went back to the moon now, could you stop them?"

"I should need some help—and some lethal weapons."

The baroness hesitated. "There is a problem about that. The moon is international territory. I can't take action on that scale without calling a meeting of the World Security Council and that is the last thing I want to do in the circumstances."

"In that case there isn't any choice, but I must have the weapons and at least one other man. You might be able to talk Mashenko into it. He is not a fighting man, but he knows his way about the reactor area where the prisoners are and he can go back without rousing too much suspicion."

The baroness considered this for a moment. "I don't like the weapons—that's a breech of the International Agreement—but, as you say, there is no choice. I'll arrange the weapons and talk to Mashenko when he arrives, but there is something you have to do first. I want the gang in the Game Park picked up and only you know where to find them. I have arranged for the warden to send a plane to collect you."

An hour later Hanson was speeding northwards over the park in one of the patrol craft. The pilot was his rescuer of the day before. Ahead of them, to the north-west, the five other patrol craft were in the air, standing by to move in when the Malib group had been located. His companion had the light of battle in her eye.

"Are these people dangerous?"

"Yes—very."

"Good—we don't get much excitement here, hardly ever get a chance to put our training to the test. I hope they don't give up too easily." When they came to the river he had swum across she brought the heliplane down to two hundred feet and made a pass along it until they found the point where he had made his crossing. A few minutes later they were over the ruined farmhouse. It was deserted. They circled the area and were beginning to gain height to start their search when Hanson called out, "There's something down there," and pointed to a dark shape lying at the edge of a clearing. When they were over it they saw that it was a human body, half concealed in the undergrowth. They put the plane down in the clearing and approached the body cautiously, stun-rays at the ready. As they came near a large black bird rose from it and flapped heavily away. Hanson grasped the legs and pulled the body clear of the brambles, and then he almost vomited. There was a gaping hole in the chest, revealing splintered ribs, and blood oozed slowly over the tattered remains of the tunic. The eyes, staring blankly at the sky, were those of Charlie, his erstwhile captor. The girl, white-faced, whispered in awe, "What on earth did that?"

"An old-fashioned shotgun I imagine, the sort sportsmen still use for small game. Both barrels at once by the look of it. Our friends are apparently more dangerous than we thought."

A further search revealed the body of Barney, or rather what he assumed was the body of Barney. His face had been shot away and he was an even ghastlier sight than Charlie. Hanson felt the body. "It's still warm—they can't be far away."

"How right you are," said a voice behind them. Hanson whirled round to see the man Baker grinning triumphantly, a shotgun pointed towards them.

"Drop those toy guns and move away from them." They did as they were told and Baker picked up the stun-rays, tucking them inside his tunic.

"Now keep walking, slowly, along that path. One wrong move and I'll blow your head off—yours, I mean, Mr Hanson," he sneered. "We have other ideas for the girl. My men will know what to do with her."

Hanson noted that he had used his name which had not come up in their previous encounter. It could only mean that Baker had been in touch with someone who knew that he, Hanson, had been dumped in the park. That seemed to imply that Malib had been responsible for his kidnapping, but it didn't make sense. Why dump him in the park when there was a chance that he might run into their group?—unless of course they thought they had killed him. Even so, why should they have wanted him out of the way? So far as he knew, only his mother and Judge Cooper knew of his interest in Malib.

That would have to wait for an answer. The immediate problem was how to get out of their present predicament before Baker met up with the rest of his party. He had no illusions about escaping from them a second time and Baker was a very different proposition from his late comrades. There was a gleam of revolutionary zeal in his eyes, almost of fanaticism, and he carried himself like a man who had trained for his task.

The girl, who was walking in front, suddenly stumbled and fell full length along the path. Hanson moved forward to help her, but Baker called out, "Stay where you are: let her get up by herself."

After about ten minutes' walk they came to a small clearing where Baker ordered them to stop and sit down on the ground. He seated himself on a fallen tree trunk and cradled the gun in his arms, but kept his finger inside the trigger guard.

Hanson turned to the girl. "How long before the others start looking for us?"

"Not long. They knew we were landing to investigate the body. If we don't get in touch with them soon they'll get suspicious and come after us. They know our position."

As she spoke she slipped her hand inside her tunic. Baker cut in, "They'll be too late." He glanced at his watch. "My men will be here in a few minutes—you won't get away this time. Heliplanes will never find us in the forest."

He pointed his gun in the air and fired one shot. "That will fetch them." Moments later there was an answering shot but they could not tell how far away it was.

What followed, happened so quickly that Hanson was taken by surprise. The girl pointed above Baker's head and shouted, "There they are." The next moment Baker was on the ground and the girl had sprung on him. A swift kick to the back of his head and it was all over. She grinned, "I picked a stone up when I pretended to trip back there—I was always good at throwing things." A dark bruise spreading across Baker's forehead showed where the stone had struck him. They dragged him into the undergrowth and the girl said, "They will probably come along the paths. You take one and I'll take the other." Hanson was surprised to find himself obeying her as if it were the most natural thing in the world.

They retrieved their stun-rays and crouched in the bushes where they could command the entrances. They did not have long to wait. The first man fell to Hanson and in seconds was unconscious and pulled into the undergrowth. Four others followed at intervals and each was silently and neatly disposed of. No more appeared and they thought they had them all when they heard voices—at least two were approaching together. Hanson moved swiftly across the clearing to join the girl. She grinned at him and whispered, "Wait until they are in the open—then we can take them together."

The voices came nearer and two men and a woman stepped out into the clearing. Hanson recognized the woman who had been arrested at the football match. She said, "There's nobody here—where have they gone?"

She was standing with a man on either side. All three were carrying shotguns. Hanson and the girl fired simultaneously and both men dropped. The woman, not knowing where the attack had come from, swung round wildly, her gun poised ready. Hanson took aim, but the girl pushed his arm down and shook her head. She waited until the woman had turned her back to her and then sprang. There was a brief struggle and the woman was on her back, First Officer Wilson on top of her, squeezing her throat with both hands.

"How many of you are there? Answer or I'll choke you." She relaxed her grip slightly and the woman gasped, "Eight." The girl released her and stood up. "I'd better call the others—we'll need some help to move this lot." She pulled a small radio transmitter from her pocket. Hanson stared at her.

"You mean to say you could have called them up at any time?"

"Yes, but then I would have missed all this. You don't know how frustrating it is to be trained for action that never comes."

"You've certainly put it to good use now. By the way, you had better tell me your first name. I can't keep calling you First Officer Wilson all the time."

"It's Sarah—Sarah Jane, after my grandmother. I'm afraid I must have been a disappointment to her. She wanted me to be an architect like herself and my mother, but the creative gene didn't survive to the third generation. I had an ancestor who was killed in the Second Feminist Revolution—I think I must be a throw-back to her."

She indicated their prisoner. "That's probably why I hate women like her so much. I can't understand how any woman could want to destroy what we fought for generations to achieve. They ought to be destroyed themselves."

The woman, who was still sitting on the ground fingering her neck, snarled up at her, "It's you who will be destroyed—you and all the others like you who pander to the matricians. You haven't been fighting for the Feminist Revolution—you've been fighting to keep the matricians in power, to keep them living in their country houses while the rest of us are shut up in the towns.

"You think you have won a great victory, capturing a handful of us here, but you're mistaken. We're only a small part—it can go on without us. We are after a much bigger target than a few matrician houses. You'll see—and it won't be long now."

"What target?"

"You'll find out soon enough and then it will be too late."

"I intend to find out now."

She sprang suddenly on the woman and pinned her to the ground, finding her throat with her hands. "I'm going to choke you to death if you don't tell me." She put pressure on her windpipe, slowly increasing it until the woman's face began to turn purple and she was beating a tattoo on the ground with her hands. She relaxed the pressure and the woman spat in her face. "That was your last chance. I'm going to kill you now." Her voice was terrifyingly calm and matter-of-fact, and she began to squeeze again. The woman beat the ground violently and a strangled attempt at speech issued from her throat. Sarah released her and the woman gasped, "The moon . . . they're . . . going to capture the moon."

Hanson intervened. "How do you know? The others did not—why should they have told you?"

The woman hesitated and Sarah took a step towards her.

"My husband, he's a footballer . . . he's there now . . . lots of others too . . . you can't stop them now . . . he told me before he got himself arrested."

The woman sat up. Long purple bruises had appeared on her neck and she cupped her hands round them, rocking to and fro in pain.

Hanson said, "I see now what you mean about being a throw-back to your ancestor. I'm glad I'm on your side. I thought for a moment you were going to kill her."

"I'm almost sorry she didn't give me the excuse." Then she remembered. "We haven't asked her where their base is. That could save us a lot of time." She turned to the woman who croaked, still with her hands round her neck, "No . . . No . . . I don't know where it is . . . Baker took us a different way each time . . . it's an old ruin with trees round it and branches for a roof . . . you can't see it until you are right at it."

She proved to be right. An hour's search of the area by all six patrol craft failed to reveal it and they returned to the park headquarters without adding to their bag of revolutionaries.

Seated in her office, the Baroness Alicia listened to what her son had to say and remained deep in thought for some time. "I am going to call a meeting of the World Security Council—I have no option now. You had better get ready to go back to the moon as soon as possible. I'll agrrange for weapons to be provided and a team to go with them. Call the Space Transport office and arrange a special flight for this evening. After that you can go and talk to your friends."

In the hall he met Fiona and Mashenko. "Nikolai, you're coming back to the moon to-night—I'll explain all about it, but I have a call to make first."

There was no reply to Hughes's private number and he keyed the public one. The same secretary as before appeared on the screen.

"Mr Hughes left early this morning on a special flight to visit the Alpha satellites. There have been complaints that supplies of ores from the asteroid belt have been delayed and he has gone to investigate. His assistant is dealing with things in his absence."

The assistant turned out to be a young man, not long out

of university and anxious to please, but staggered at the thought of arranging a special flight off his own bat. After an assurance that he would receive confirmation from the baroness herself, he agreed to put the arrangements in hand.

Mashenko was waiting for him in the hall with Fiona beside him, both agog with curiosity. "What's been happening? Why are we going back to the moon?"

"All in good time—I'll tell you about it over lunch. All this rampaging about in the Game Park has given me an appetite."

Over the table he told them the story of the last three days, leaving out some of the gory details for Fiona's benefit. When he came to the part where they escaped from Baker and captured the rest of the gang he did not trouble to conceal his admiration for Sarah and her exploits. Fiona said nothing but he was aware of a slight stiffening in her manner, almost as if she were jealous. At least, that was what he hoped it implied. When he came to the end of the story he turned to Mashenko.

"There is no question about it now; Malib are going to try to capture the moon. Therefore, Nikolai, you and I are going there to-night with a contingent of police and we are going to make sure they don't."

"Why me? I am a scientist, not a fighting man. I have never used a weapon in my life."

"You didn't do so badly with that chair leg at the football match. Anyway, it's unlikely you'll have to do any fighting. That's what the police are for. We need someone who is familiar with the reactor and laboratory complex and we can't count on using any of the other staff. Some of them may have gone over to Malib. There must be some fairly senior people involved somewhere along the line."

He turned to Fiona. "And now I am going to return Fiona's compliment and show her our gardens while you get some aiming practice in the Games Room—there are some practice pistols and targets there."

They were still in the garden when the first intercontinental hydrojet set itself down gently on the landing-pad, bearing in its sleek tritinium body Mme. Drasa Lubinka, African member of the World Security Council. She had been settling down for an afternoon siesta on the *stoep* of her house on the mountainside overlooking Table Bay when the summons arrived, and was not at all pleased by it. Strikingly tall, almost six feet, with the magnificent carriage of her far distant Zulu ancestors, she was impressive at any time, the more so when she was angry, as she undoubtedly was now. She strode towards the house, impatiently brushing aside the manservant who was waiting to help her down from her plane. Still only in her thirties, she was the youngest member of the council and had a reputation for direct frankness that was unusual in a politician. Watching her cross the lawn, Hanson said to Fiona. "There is one member of the council who does not look too pleased. I'm afraid my mother is going to have a rough time."

The next to arrive was Wallis K Vanderbilt, Vice-President of the Americas. She had been sitting down to breakfast when her secretary came in with the message. She finished it in comfort before ordering her hydrojet. Though not quite so tall as Mme. Lubinka, she was none the less an imposing figure of a woman. Like the baroness, she was in her early fifties but did not look it. Her smooth, unlined features looked as if they had been chiselled from the same piece of alabaster as her carefully sculpted hair which was speckled with grey. She recognized Hanson who was crossing the lawn as she came up with him.

"Well, Roger, it sure is nice to see you, but I just hope Alicia hasn't gotten me here on some wild-goose chase. I've had to cancel three meetings and an appointment with my dentist to get here."

She neither waited for an answer nor asked to be introduced to Fiona, who, although used to moving in high circles, was a little overawed by the importance of the visitors.

Last to arrive was Mrs Hilda Kritzinger, Vice-President of Australasia. Unlike the others, she had not been at home when the summons came. She had been holidaying in Switzerland and it had taken some time to locate the mountain chalet where she had been enjoying the attentions of a handsome climbing instructor. She, needless to say, was the most annoyed of all at the interruption. Quite clearly it was going to be a difficult meeting.

They were sitting on the terrace in the afternoon sunshine when one of the baroness's secretaries came to fetch him. Fiona had just said, "You know, it's strange how people keep disappearing—first you, then Alaric. He was to escort me yesterday but didn't turn up. I called him at his flat and then at the Guards' mess but no-one seemed to know where he was." Her remark was forgotten in what followed and it was only much later that its significance was to dawn on him.

The atmosphere in the baroness's office was highly charged to say the least. Hanson found himself confronted by the unwavering stare of four pairs of eyes whose owners were seated at a semicircular conference table. His mother, as befitted the Chairman of the Council, sat in the centre. It reminded Hanson of his first interview as a candidate for the Administrative Service, only this was different. These were the second most powerful women in the world; only the heads of the four states could exercise more influence, but in matters of security these four were supreme. He stood waiting, not knowing quite what was expected of him until the American spoke. "I guess in the circumstances we can allow him to sit down, Alicia. No need to stand on ceremony."

At a nod from the baroness he brought over a chair and sat down facing them. She said, "These ladies are not convinced by what I have told them—they want to hear it from your own lips."

"Too right we're not convinced," the Australian interrupted. "There are almost a hundred men on the moon, not counting the prisoners, and you are asking us to believe that a dozen footballers, unarmed, can overpower their guards and then travel three hundred miles across the moon and capture the main base. Having done that, these footballers are then going to get control of the world."

"Let him speak, Hilda," interrupted Mme Lubinka. "We all know why you are in a hurry to get away."

The Australian sat back with a gesture of impatience and shot a venomous glance at her dark-skinned colleague.

Hanson resisted the temptation to confront the hot-tempered Australian and instead turned to Mme. Lubinka whom he sensed to be more reasonable.

"I agree the evidence is rather thin and, if it were not for the woman in the Game Park, I would be inclined to doubt it myself."

Mme. Lubinka countered, "The woman is the only hard evidence you've got—the rest is mere supposition. Besides, you got her evidence under duress. She may well have invented it on the spur of the moment to avoid being choked to death—I know I would have thought up something."

"I hardly think so. The idea is too fantastic for her to have invented it—and there is her husband." He turned to his mother. "Have you had him checked out?"

"Yes, he was sent to the moon two months ago."

Hanson, still addressing himself to the African, went on, "That at least confirms part of her story. I don't think we can afford to assume the rest of it was a fiction. Then there are the people in the park. We know that they were going to attack some unspecified matrician houses."

His mother interrupted, "The man Baker was questioned and I had a report from the police. They were going to attack this house and Baroness Cunningham's." Baroness Cunningham was Deputy Governor of Britian. "The signal for the attack was to be a pattern of flares dropped over the park. I'm afraid the police were a little too enthusiastic in their questioning. Baker died from an overdose of Veritin before they could learn any more."

The tall Zulu, whose eyes had never left Hanson's face since he started talking, spoke up now. "Suppose your inference is correct, I find it hard to believe that a handful of football players could carry it out. As Mrs Kritzinger said, there are almost a hundred men on the moon."

"I think I see how it could be done. The warders would not be expecting an attack. They are there, not to guard the convicts, but to see that they get to the tunnelling area and work when they get there.

"At the start of the work-day they are taken to the Tunnelling Control building where they are issued with space-suits under the superivision of six warders who are armed with stun-rays and electronic goads. The suits are checked back in the same way at the end of the day and then the prisoners are taken by railcar to their quarters where they are sealed in. Without space-suits they would die as soon as they opened the airlock. You must remember that, even if they could overpower the warders, they have no incentive to escape. There is no way they could get away from the moon.

"It becomes quite a different proposition if you have a bunch of determined men with a definite objective. There are twelve professional footballers there now—men whose livelihood depends on being able to maim or even kill their opponents with no weapons but their hands and feet. Half a dozen unsuspecting guards would be no match for them. Having overpowered the warders they would have no trouble in dealing with the laboratory staff. Then, armed with the warders' stun-rays, they could travel to the main base in the routine monorail car. Once there, I don't see how they could be stopped. The only weapons there would be the guns of the off-duty guards and they would be locked in the armoury."

The four women continued to regard him. Mme. Lubinka was the first to speak. "I'm convinced—I think we should do something about it. How about you, Wallis?" She turned to the American who replied, "I guess that's good enough for me. Thing is, what do we aim to do about it?"

The baroness, in control of the situation once more, said, "That is already organized. My son here and Nikolai Mashenko, a Russian physicist, will leave for the moon to-night with a detachment of police who will be armed with something better than stun-rays—portable cutting lasers fitted into stun-ray bodies. The suspect convicts will be collected and brought back here for questioning."

Her Excellency Hilda Kritzinger was not to be put off so easily. Still smarting under the earlier rebuke, she complained, "That won't do at all, Alicia. We have had enough of your high-handedness to-day. You know the rule about the moon—no unilateral action. Any force sent to the moon must be an international one; equal numbers from all of us and a commander chosen by ballot. I won't go along with this—you had no right to make any arrangements without consulting the rest of us. I move that we each provide a quarter of the force and that we appoint a commander by ballot—not a Eurasian. We all know where the trouble started. We must have a commander we can trust."

There was a stunned silence—open insults were almost unheard of in feminine diplomacy. Then Mme. Lubinka, who had been watching Hanson's face during this outburst said quietly, "I think Mr Hanson here may have some views about that."

A visiphone buzzed on the baroness's desk and she rose to answer it. Hanson said, "Mme. Lubinka is right. By to-night at the latest, Malib will know that we have rounded up their gang in the Game Park and that we are on to them. They can't be sure that we have not discovered their plan to capture the moon. My guess is that they will put it into operation as soon as they can. We have no time to make up an international force. We may be too late even now."

"I'm afraid we are too late." The baroness, her face grey and drawn, walked slowly down from her desk holding a piece of paper in her hand.

"This has just been relayed from the moon: 'Attention all World Governments. This message comes to you from the Revolutionary Council of the Organization for Male Liberation. We have taken over the moon and are in full command. In one hour from now we shall cut off power supplies to London, Washington, Capetown and Sydney. Two hours later they will be restored and there will be a further announcement'."

The baroness slumped heavily into her chair and sat staring blankly at the sheet of paper. It was the Australian who first broke the silence. Her voice was subdued now and all the angry arrogance had gone from it as she addressed herself to Hanson.

"This doesn't change anything does it, except that it makes your task more difficult? Will you need a larger force?"

Hanson said slowly, "I'm afraid it makes it impossible. The shuttle service from the earth only goes as far as the transit satellite. Movement from there is controlled from the moon."

"Can't a shuttle go direct from here without touching the satellite?"

"No, the whole transport system is designed to make the moon almost impregnable. The shuttles rely on gravity-reversal drive units and are arranged for remote control from within the gravity field in which they happen to be. Once they enter the moon's field they are controlled from there."

"They can be modified, surely?"

Hanson shook his head. "They are built entirely, drive units as well, on Alpha Three satellite which we can't reach either. Even if we were to set up facilities on the earth it would take too long to do it." He paused for a moment. "These people are not fools. I expect that by now all available shuttles are in the moon's gravitational field, in which case there is no way of bringing one back."

It took ten minutes to verify that the last shuttle entered the moon's gravitational field half an hour before the Malib message was received.

"We're finished, then?" the Australian said, looking from one to the other and back to Hanson again. No-one answered. Hanson wondered what thoughts were going through their minds. His mother, some colour returned to her cheeks, but still looking strained, was staring in front of her, absently tapping the table with her hand. Her Excellency Wallis K. Vanderbilt was thoughtfully working a slim ivory toothpick between her front teeth and the Australian sat with her head in her hands, gazing at the table as if she expected to see a vision of the future reflected in the highly polished mahogany. Only the African appeared to be unaffected. She sat erect like an ebony statue as she had done throughout the meeting, her features inscrutable except for the coal-black eyes which burned with dark intensity. When she spoke her rich, husky voice was perfectly calm.

"There must be some way—we can't simply give up."

"I'm afraid the only way would be to build a space-ship from scratch on the earth and that would be almost impossible. All our design experts are based on Alpha Three. It must be nearly a century and a half since any sort of space vehicle was built under earth-gravity conditions."

"Say—wait a minute. Maybe little ol' America can save you all yet."

All eyes turned towards Wallis K Vanderbilt who had removed her toothpick and was describing tiny circles with it in the air.

"We've got the very thing at Cape Kennedy Space Museum—the last moon rocket that was ever built. I remember being taken to see it when I was a child, a great shining thing sticking up into the sky. There was a great little guy who looked after it—you'd almost think he'd given birth to it. He knew just about everything there was to know about it. Reckoned he could still get it up to the moon if he had to. I guess you girls had better adjourn while I get on to Washington."

Hanson was alone with Fiona when the summons came for him to return to his mother's office. The four women were seated at the table in the same positions as when he had last entered the room, but their attitude had undergone a subtle change. They still looked as if they were trying to assess him, but with the air of people who were about to ask a favour and were not sure that it would be granted. His mother was the first to speak.

"They have carried out their threat: London, Washington, Capetown and Sydney are on emergency power supplies and all work has come to a stop. Only essential services are operating and one holoscreen channel has been kept open in each town. Luckily most of the workers were able to get home before the transport systems were shut down."

She paused to give more emphasis to what she had to say next.

"The moon-rocket at Cape Kennedy will be ready for launching in twenty-four hours. The actual launch time will be somewhere in the following twenty-four hours, depending on where it is decided to make the landing. There is, however, a small snag."

"Hell," cut in Wallis K Vanderbilt. "You English and your understatements. The small snag," she turned to Hanson, "is that it can only carry three people."

The baroness acknowledged the interruption with the merest lift of an eyebrow.

"There is no need to get emotional about it—we don't even know if it can be done, but it is our only chance. Do you think, Roger," and her voice softened a little on his name, "that if it is possible, you would be one of the three?" She let her hands fall to the table and leaned back in her chair. This pleading gesture, so unlike her, disconcerted him and he walked over to the window where he stood looking out on the garden for a long time.

When he turned to face them they were all wearing a look of anxious expectancy and he felt he ought to savour the moment. These women of power and influence were at his mercy. It was a strange sensation and one he was never likely to know again. He spoke slowly as if judicially measuring each word before he pronounced it.

"I think it might be possible for three people to pull it off and, as you say, it is our only chance. Yes, I'm prepared to try but I shall need Mashenko—I'm not familiar enough with the reactor complex and our only chance is to capture it first."

A sigh of relief went up and his mother said, "I'll talk to Nikolai," in a tone that made him wonder if there was something between them. "Who will be the third person?"

"I think." he said, "I would like First Officer Wilson from the Game Park control."

"That can be arranged—if she is prepared to take the risk."

Hanson permitted himself a smile, "I think she will."

He was right. Two hours later she arrived, bubbling over with excitement and not a little awed by her surroundings. Matrician houses did not figure largely on her visiting list. "I'll never be able to thank you enough," she gasped. "You should have seen the others' faces when they heard—they were quite green."

"You had better save your thanks until you see what you have let yourself in for. Come with me and I'll show you."

He led her into a small anteroom off the hall. Set out on a table which almost filled the room were models of two sections of the moon's surface. On one of these was a small-scale replica of the moon-base itself which had been put together from photographs by one of the baroness's assistants. On the other was a similar model of the reactor complex including the laboratory and the prison quarters. This one had been constructed from Mashenko's memory and was not quite so accurately conceived.

Mashenko came in to join them, a worried expression on his open Slav countenance. Of the three he was the least suited to an enterprise of this kind. Hanson had no doubts about the girl; she had already shown what she could do in a tight corner. As for himself, he had survived the Spartan rigours of an educational system which had the reputation of being the toughest in the world, a system in which physical endurance and self-reliance were venerated almost as much as intellectual ability. The Russian by contrast, had spent most of his life behind desks or laboratory benches and had not even played competitive games at school. Now he was about to be plunged into an expedition which might well cost him his life. Hanson wondered, not for the first time, how his mother had managed to persuade him.

"I want you," he began, "to study this model carefully and memorize the positions of the different buildings. It will be night on this side of the moon when we land and everything will be in darkness.

"Our first objective is the reactor complex which is three hundred miles from moon-base itself. The complex has no sleeping accommodation, except, of course for the prison quarters, and all the staff return to the main base at the end of the working day. Only the reactor control room, the rectangular extension at the end of the laboratory building is manned permanently. There are four men on duty who work in four-hour shifts. There are two airlocks on this building. The one on your left is the docking-bay for the monorail car which transports passengers to and from the main base. It opens only when the railcar docks into it.

"The other one here, which we shall have to use, can be opened from the outside provided the inner door is closed. When the outer door is open a warning light is displayed above the inner one and another in the security room. The security room is midway between the airlock and the reactor control room. It is not usually manned outside normal working hours but we can't count on that. They are almost certain to have some sort of guard on watch with the duty controllers.

"Provided we can get into the building we should not have too much trouble dealing with the guard. What we do after that will depend on what we learn from the controllers, always assuming they are still on our side."

"How do we get into the main base?"

"Quite frankly, I don't know yet. There are only two possible ways. Either we travel back in the monorail car which brings the relief controllers, or we use one of the emergency hydrojets which are kept there in case of a breakdown on the monorail. We shall have to decide that when we know what the set-up is at the other end. I've had a detailed plan of the base transmitted from London. You, Sarah, will have to memorize that as well"

When he had finished there was silence for a time. Now that they had got down to details, the more Hanson thought about it the crazier it seemed. Here they were, two men and a girl setting off to attack a base occupied by almost a hundred people, and no idea of what they were really up against. There were twenty-one suspect convicts—and there their knowledge stopped. They had no way of telling how many of the base staff might have gone over to Malib and, worst of all, they did not know who their leader was. It might be any one of the men he had worked with over the last two years. They would not be able to tell friend from foe until perhaps it was too late.

Sarah Wilson alone showed no sign of anxiety. While the two men stood contemplating the near impossibility of what they were about to attempt, she was wholly absorbed in studying the layout of the buildings.

It was still only late afternoon in Florida when the hydrojet slid gently to a halt on the flat expanse of the old launching-ground at Cape Kennedy. The rocket towered above it like an enormous finger pointing at the sky, gleaming in the afternoon sunshine through a lattice-work of scaffolding. Parked alongside it was a mobile platform on which they could distinguish figures moving about.

"Is that it?" asked Sarah. "Isn't it huge?—I didn't dream it would be so big. You could get a hundred people in it—so why only three of us?"

Mashenko, who had been reading it up in Malinovsky's *History of Space Flight*, explained. "It is two hundred and seventy feet long, but only the last forty feet or so is usable space and most of that is taken up by instruments and primitive life support systems. The rest is fuel tanks and rocket motors, twelve of them in three stages plus one in the space-ship itself. Allowing for inflation, that machine cost more than fifty times as much as the shuttles we use to-day and all of it, except for a tiny return capsule, is thrown away. Most of what you see will have been jettisoned by the time we leave the earth's gravity field."

They were spared a long lecture by the arrival, in a hovercar, of the museum director, a plump, fussy little man in his fifties with thinning grey hair, who spoke in jerky staccato sentences. He introduced himself, "John P Tyzak, Museum Director. Glad to make your acquaintance. We'll go to my office. There are people waiting to see you. Terrible business, this—don't know whether I'm coming or going—people rushing about all over the place. Heaven knows what this is going to cost, not to speak of losing our finest exhibit. I don't know who is going to pay for this—can't come out of my budget."

Hanson was amazed. Here they were in the midst of the worst crisis the world had known for nearly two centuries and all this little man could think about was his budget. He hoped the flight arrangements were in other hands. John P Tyzak was not the man to inspire confidence.

There were only two people waiting for them in the director's office. A tall, broad-shouldered man rose to greet them with a smile that seemed to stretch from ear to ear. He stretched out a huge hand. "Jefferson Diefenbaker, Presidential Special Assistant, pleased to meet you." He turned to the woman seated at the director's desk. "Let me introduce

Mrs. Martha Johnson, White House Chief of Staff."

She did not get up, nor did she hold out her hand. "The President has appointed Mr Diefenbaker here to take charge of this operation. I am here at the President's special request to make sure that you get everything you need with the least possible delay." She made it quite clear that she regarded this as being beneath her but that a mere man could not be left to issue orders to all and sundry, "The President has asked me to convey to you her deep appreciation of the risks you are taking and to wish you success in your mission." With that she signified that her contribution to the discussion was at an end and, as if to show that she had more important matters to deal with, resumed her study of an impressive-looking document in a folder bearing what Hanson recognized as the Presidential Seal.

He breathed a sigh of relief—a man would be easier to deal with. Diefenbaker said, "First of all I reckon you could use some of our American hospitality right now—Mr Director, why don't you open that cupboard of yours and pour us all out a drink?" The director grudgingly complied—no doubt making a mental reservation to exclude it from his budget at the same time. When each had been settled with the drink of his or her choice—the White House Chief of Staff declined—Diefenbaker went on, "I guess you are wondering how you are going to learn to fly that little old rocket out there with only twenty-four hours to go. Well, I have news for you—we've gotten you a pilot."

He went to the door, opened it and called out, "Jimmy, come and meet your passengers."

To say that they were totally unprepared for what emerged from the corridor was an understatement so gross that the most phlegmatic of Englishmen would not have dared to perpetrate it. The memory of it was to stay with them for the rest of their lives.

A wizened little man with a shock of pure white hair stepped smartly into the room. He must have been at least seventy. Only the bright eyes and the quick, birdlike movements gave an impression of boyish eagerness which belied his appearance. All three contemplated him in stunned silence.

"Folks, let me introduce Jimmy Chapman who knows more about the Saturn rockets than any man alive." Diefenbaker sounded for all the world like a showman introducing the star performer of the evening.

"I must admit that when we dug him out of his retirement village in Orlando we had no idea of sending him up with you. After all, he retired five years ago, and even then he was well over the age. But Jimmy persuaded us—he's just about the most persuasive little guy I've ever met. He talked us into giving him a medical and, what do you know, the best space medics in America voted him one hundred percent fit to make the trip. After that we just had to give in."

The little man stood smiling in front of them, glancing from one to the other, his bright little eyes taking everything in. This, Hanson realized, must be the vice-president's 'great little guy' who knew everything there was to know about the rocket.

How much he knew they discovered when he began to talk. His knowledge was not limited to the rocket itself and its complex instrumentation. In early youth he had been fascinated by the stories of the space pioneers blasting off into the unknown in their primitive machines and he had read everything he could find on the subject. In his spare time he had mastered the mathematics of space navigation and he talked of trajectories, circular and parabolic orbits and Kepler's Harmonic Law. His work at the museum had clearly been a labour of love and it seemed as if his whole life had been a preparation for this moment. In all the years he had lovingly tended the ancient rocket he had never dreamed that one day he would take off in it. The fact that the object of his life-long care would shortly, except for a tiny section, be jettisoned into empty space did not appear to dismay him.

He was, as Diefenbaker had said, a very persuasive little guy and by the time he had finished they were left with no doubts about the capabilities of their pilot; they could not have been in better hands.

"I must go back to the rocket now—there are hundreds of checks to be carried out before morning and some of them I want to do myself. Before I go, there is one thing I need to know. Whereabouts on the moon do you want to make your landing?"

"Near the reactor complex."

"Good. I have a trajectory and final moon orbit that will do just that. I'll feed it into the base computer now and it will give us the actual launch time. It should be sometime to-morrow afternoon."

Hanson blinked. "But how . . . in the time?"

The little man grinned apologetically. "A man has to have a hobby when he retires. This has been mine. I have flight paths and approximate launch times worked out for every day on which moon flights are possible for the next three years. It was simply a case of going to my files and extracting to-morrow's. They are designed to match in with the programming of the old NASA computer which, like everything else here, has been maintained in its original working order."

He turned to go, then stopped at the door. "Say, I nearly forgot, Mr Diefenbaker—the operating instructions and diagrams for the mooncraft are being processed into three hypnopaedic machines and should be ready in about an hour." The next instant he had disappeared through the door.

When he had gone Diefenbaker grinned wryly. "Jimmy sure has got it all sewn up—reckon you don't need me around any more. All that's left for me is to show you to the flat the director has put at your disposal. I'll have the sleep-teachers sent over when they arrive. I guess you won't need to adjust for jet-lag since you'll be back on Greenwich time when you hit the moon."

As they were about to leave the White House Chief of Staff took Hanson aside. "We've had another message from the moon. They want us to submit for their approval lists of names from which to choose all-male provisional governments. We have been given twenty-four hours to reply. After that we are to receive further instructions. If we do not comply they will cut off all power supplies until we do. That would mean that every city in the world would be without food, water or sanitation. The sociologists estimate that at best we could not hold out for more than three days. After that it would be everyone for himself—killing and looting on a wide scale. We have no choice but to go along with them. Our only hope is that you can get to them before things reach the point where we can't reverse them."

She had no need to say more. Hanson could picture for himself the chaos that would follow the power cuts. Once Satellite Solar Power Stations had been established in permanent orbit to beam down unlimited supplies of cheap electricity the cities of the world had become totally dependent on them. Sleep and sex apart, there was scarcely any human activity that could be carried on without a vast consumption of electrical energy. Food was produced, cooked and distributed by an intricate network of computer-controlled robot processors. In the vast honeycombs of living modules in the large cities even the very air they breathed was supplied by electrical circulatory systems. The sociologists, as usual, had got their sums wrong. In three days most of the population would either have asphyxiated in their homes or broken out into the surrounding countryside where eventually they would die of starvation. Killing and looting would only be the beginning. It would be followed by mass starvation and, in the end, urestrained cannibalism. It was not a pretty picture.

Hanson could not sleep. For the third time he removed the padded skull-cap of the hypnopaedic machine from his head and got out of bed. The wall clock told him that it was only an hour since he had first turned in. It seemed longer. Outside it was still early evening and the bright Florida sunshine was sneaking into the room through the ventilator shaft. Birds were singing and somewhere a robot grass-cutting machine was whirring away its endless programme. He switched on the light and picked up a book but could not get interested in it. Then he began pacing the room but that was no use—it was too small. He wondered if the others were asleep or were they too victims of the same restlessness. Eventually he slipped on a pair of shorts and went out into the living area. Three of the room's four walls were of glass and unshuttered. Sunlight streamed through one end and through the other he looked out over the low flat-roofed buildings of the museum to the east where the Atlantic provided a deep blue shimmering backdrop.

From Mashenko's room came the faint hum of the hypnopaedic machine. He at least was fast asleep. No sound came from the girl's room; perhaps her machine was between cycles. He wondered if the old-time astronauts had felt like this on the night before blast-off or whether they had slept as soundly as Mashenko was apparently sleeping now.

He would pour himself a drink and then, if that did not work, he would take one of the Hypnomathin pills which Diefenbaker had provided. He did not normally use them. At school he had discovered that he retained a much clearer picture of the night's instruction without them, something odd in his brain chemistry he supposed.

Diefenbaker, deprived by little Jimmy of his main responsibility, the rocket and the flight itself, had gone to town on the creature comforts of the participants. A lavishly supplied tray of drinks stood on a table by the window. Hanson selected a rare malt whisky and, reluctantly, because there was nothing else, added some chilled water from a crystal jug. He must have made a noise in the process because a door opened and Sarah Wilson emerged.

"Oh, it's you Mr Hanson, I thought . . ."

"I don't think we can go through the next few days addressing each other as First Officer Wilson and Mr Hanson—too much of a mouthful for operational efficiency. We had better be Roger and Sarah. Would you like a drink?"

"Yes, please Mr . . . sorry . . . Roger. I can't get to sleep. I took one of those Hypnomathin pills, but every time I put the thing on my head I come wide awake."

"My trouble too," he smiled. "Let's see what a drink will do. The old-time astronauts will probably turn in their graves—they didn't touch alcohol for weeks before a flight."

He poured her a drink and they stood looking out towards the sea. Whether it was the drink or that subtle blend of intimacy that is induced by a shared adventure, Hanson could never afterwards decide. They stood in silence for a time and it was not until she spoke that he realized that for the last few minutes he had been aware of nothing but her presence beside him.

"Isn't it strange to think that this time to-morrow we'll be up there, hurtling through the air at eighteen thousand miles an hour?"

"Are you scared?"

"No, only . . . Oh, Roger . . ." and she turned towards him.

Afterwards, lying in his bed, she said drowsily, "I read somewhere once that people do this when . . . when they feel they may not have long to live. Do you think that's what it was with us?"

"No—not like that . . . we were too close . . . it was more than that."

"I'm not so sure . . . I would like to have your baby . . . I didn't take any precautions."

He said nothing, but held her very tightly.

Hanson's first action on awakening was to check the indicator on the sleep-teacher. It had completed only three cycles, one short of the number normally required. The moment of waking after a hypnopaedic session was always the same. For some reason one expected to find some trace of it lingering in the mind like a half-remembered dream, but there never was. The only thing that distinguished it from an ordinary awakening was a preternatural freshness and clarity as if one had been purged in a sort of mental Turkish bath. There was only one way to check it. He ran a bath, lay back in it with his eyes closed and formed a thought image of the mooncraft. Ten minutes later he sat up and washed himself. The diagrams and operating instructions had come through as clearly as if he had known them all his life.

When he came out the others were already at breakfast. He was relieved to note that Sarah greeted him casually as if nothing had happened between them. It was not that he had feelings of guilt or anything like that. It had come about so naturally and simply that it seemed no more than a fitting prelude to what was to come. But he was not sure how Mashenko would react if he suspected. His escapade with Leonora, which he had not mentioned once since Hanson's return, had done nothing to soften the streak of puritanism that ran through him. It might have undermined his morale to think that on the night before a hazardous enterprise his companions had been cavorting between the sheets. Looking at Sarah now, he found it difficult to believe that it had really happened. She was as she had always been, a highly trained fighting woman, and was discussing the weapons they were to use. The guns were being modified in London and would not be delivered until later in the morning.

Before they had finished eating the 'great little guy' arrived. "Morning, folks. Ready for the next stage?" He must have been up half the night but he was as fresh and eager as he had been the evening before. He had brought with him a small projector and some slides.

"First of all I want to show you the flight path we checked

out on the computer. Blast-off, if you folks will excuse the old-fashioned term will be at fifteen-fourteen this afternoon. The circle on the left of the screen is the earth and the one on the right is the moon.

"You will see that we start by going into orbit around the earth about one and a quarter times. That is to get us launched on the trajectory we need to take us to the right point on the moon at the right time.

"At this point here the first stage rocket that takes us off the ground is jettisoned. The second stage takes over then and we accelerate into orbit at a little under eighteen thousand miles an hour. At point number two here it burns out and is jettisoned like the first stage. Then we continue in orbit until we reach point three where we fire the third stage. That takes us up to twenty-five thousand miles an hour—enough to take us out of the earth's gravity field."

He paused for a moment and his face took on a portentous expression.

"And now we come to a problem that the space pioneers did not have to face. Our trajectory takes us straight through the power beam from Satellite Solar Power Station Three.—ten million megawatts of microwave energy. We don't know what effect this will have on the ship's electrical and electronic systems and there is no way we can test it in the time.

"What we have done is to fit a modern radio unit which can be unplugged and sealed in a specially shielded box when we pass through the beam. That way we will be able to rely on the base controller if the on-board computer is knocked out.

"Our problem really starts when we slow down to five thousand miles an hour and disappear round the other side of the moon where the base can't reach us. At that point we would normally rely on the on-board computer to calculate the release point for the mooncraft in which you are going to land."

He paused again and fished a small rectangular object

from his pocket. "This is one of two micro-computers which have been programmed in parallel with the base computer and the ship's one. They will be kept in shielded boxes until we have passed the power beam. There is one for the command module and one for the mooncraft and they will both give a read-out of every operation and the count-down. They will not—and I emphasize this—they will not be able to take account of any variations to the planned trajectory or orbit. This means that we will be unable to make any corrections after we pass behind the moon and may well finish up hundreds of miles from our target."

Mashenko, unable to accept what he imagined to be a lack of precision in the calculations, asked, "Why should there be any variation in the flight path?"

Jimmy was apologetic. "Well, folks, the fact is you see, we don't know enough about this type of rocket . . ."

"I thought . . ."

"Yes, I know—you thought I knew all about it. Well, I do in a sense, but you see this type has never flown before. It was the last of the Saturn rockets to be built, a big advance on the earlier ones with improved motors and fuel and a simplified control system. The wars at the end of the twentieth century put a temporary stop to the space programme. By the time they were over we had developed much better propulsion systems and this rocket was obsolete. Rather than scrap it, they put it in mothballs and preserved it in the museum here.

"Any number of things could throw us off the planned flight path—mistakes in the original fuel calculations, delay in firing a particular stage—you name it."

Hanson chipped in, "How far could we travel in the mooncraft itself if we went off course?"

"The short answer is—not at all. The mooncraft is designed to land at a specific point and take off again into orbit. It can't be used for lateral movement on the surface. We have been able to make one modification that will help. It has been fitted with a radio-camera that will project on a screen a relief map of the area you are passing over. Once you have identified your position on the main map it will be comparatively easy to fire the braking rockets to bring you down at the point nearest the target."

All this was delivered in a propitiatory tone as if the little man was afraid that they would decide to pull out of the operation, but when he finished his face broke into a boyish smile. "That's all for now, folks. I must get back to the rocket. I had hoped to show you round it this morning but some of the tests are taking longer than we expected and you won't be able to get into the command module until an hour before blast-off. There will be plenty time for explanations once we are off. Now I suggest you find out if your weapons have arrived and get some practice in."

Jimmy's talk had not been calculated to fill them with confidence in the outcome. Mashenko in particular was sceptical about it. "I do not like it, we are leaving too much to chance. These things should be precise and accurate. How can we travel hundreds of miles in space-suits? They won't keep us alive long enough to reach the target—we shall die to no purpose. I'm going to find the flight controller."

Hanson watched him go and shrugged his shoulders. "Let's go and find our weapons."

The laser guns proved to be all they had hoped for and more. They were equipped with tiny batteries capable of firing ten five-second bursts. Each was provided with five batteries plus one spare for practice. The modifications had been expertly carried out and there was nothing to distinguish them from ordinary stun-rays except that some ingenious engineer had had the foresight to fit them with simple optical sights, a modification that had not occurred to Hanson. By the time Mashenko rejoined them he and Sarah could hit the centre of a three-inch circle at twenty-five yards with only a one-second burst. At that rate one battery would be enough to kill fifty men.

Mashenko was looking more cheerful when he returned. "He says it is not so bad. Jimmy was . . . how you say? . . .

carried away. If we are not on the correct path when we go behind the moon we can do a complete orbit so that they can signal corrections to us. This is good?"

Hanson shook his head. "No, I don't like that. A complete orbit would carry us over moonbase. They might just spot us—we can't afford to take the risk. Surprise is our only advantage. We'll face that problem when it comes."

Strapped into his seat in the command module, Hanson struggled to fight off the claustrophobia which descended on him with the closing of the hatch. It came in great waves with a sense of panic and the feeling that he could not breathe. It was not helped by the cumbersome old-fashioned space-suits they had to wear because the modern type could not be adapted to the capsule's life-support systems. They would not be able to change into their ordinary suits until they were almost at the moon. He had had some difficulty in persuading Jimmy that they had to have the simpler and lighter modern suits to fight in. There were times when the little man seemed almost to forget the purpose of the expedition and to treat it as if it were intended to be a reconstruction of an early moon flight.

In an effort to take his mind off the shut-in feeling he looked at the others. Even through the visor of his helmet, Jimmy's eyes were alive and sparkling. This was the greatest moment of his life and he was going to extract every last ounce of enjoyment from it.

Sarah and Mashenko were staring solemnly in front of them, looking strangely impersonal in their space-suits. He wondered what was going on in their minds. Now that they were irrevocably committed his own confidence had begun to wane. There had been something very final about the closing of the hatch. Doubts that he had forcibly shut off were creeping into his mind . . . the uncertain landing . . . the unknown odds . . . how they were to get into the main base. Not least, he was worried by the fact that none of them had actually killed another human being. What would happen when the moment came to squeeze the trigger?

Would they hesitate and so risk being killed themselves? What did it feel like to kill a man in cold blood?

He glanced at the count-down indicator. It showed two minutes to go. They were all watching it now. Only Jimmy's eyes were eager and expectant. The other two sat mesmerized, conscious only of the decimals whirring round so fast they could not be read and the slower, inexorable march of the seconds . . . 59 . . . 58 . . . 57 . . .

When the moment of lift-off came it was an anticlimax. At first there was nothing, simply nothing and he thought the motor had failed to fire. Then he was conscious of a slight vibration, but still no sensation of movement; all he could see through the observation port was a patch of clear blue Florida sky which appeared to be standing still. Gradually he felt the pull of gravity as the rocket accelerated. Sarah turned and gave him a nervous smile.

Then he blacked out. When he came round he saw that the others had fared no better. Jimmy was conscious, but blinking rather hard, as was Sarah. Mashenko was the last to come round and grinned apologetically as if he felt foolish. Jimmy called out over the intercom, "Different from gravity reversal, isn't it. You had to be tough in the old days."

Except to Sarah, who had never been off the earth before, and Jimmy who was in the seventh heaven, the flight was boring and monotonous, but they did have some laughs at Sarah's attempts to cope with weightlessness. Jimmy kept up a desultory conversation with the base flight controller and, in between times, tried to explain the operation of the complex instruments and controls. Much of it had been designed to collect and analyse information which was no longer needed, but Jimmy, like a schoolboy who had made a new discovery, insisted on explaining everything in minutest detail. As a retirement present, he had been given a trip to the moon a few years previously, but he had not been impressed by it; nothing like the "real thing" as he put it.

They were well out towards the moon when the ground controller's voice came through, muffled and indistinct, warning that they would be passing through the satellite beam in five minutes. Jimmy carefully unplugged the radio and inserted it in the specially shielded container as the count-down indicator began to flicker. The sense of unreality and effortless well-being induced by their weightless condition disappeared and a growing tension took its place as they watched the indicator.

When it reached zero it suddenly went mad. Random figures chased one another across the dial at incredible speed, backwards and forwards, and suddenly a mad rush backwards, seconds changing as if they were decimals, until it ended on zero and then cut out. In the few seconds it lasted they did not see what had happened to the other instruments.

Jimmy, his normal birdlike movements slowed down by weightlessness, carefully removed the radio from its shielded box and plugged it in.

"Moonflight to Base, Moonflight to Base—can you hear me?"

"Base to Moonflight—we hear you. Carry out test routines." One by one he checked the circuits and instruments and called out the results to base. All of them turned out to be functioning correctly except the cosmic ray measuring device which had gone completely dead and didn't matter anyway. The last check was to run a test programme through the computer and, although they did not understand it, the other three watched closely while Jimmy keyed in the test digits and read the results to base.

When he had finished he shouted, "Were okay, folks, we're okay—its checked out all the way. Only one thing we couldn't check—the firing circuits for the braking rockets. Reckon they didn't think they were worth bothering about—they're duplicated anyway. If they work, they work. If they don't we go right on out into space."

Hanson had a tidy mind and an almost pathological dislike of unknown quantities, but on this trip they were piling one on top of the other at such a rate that this latest one left him unmoved. He did not waste time speculating on how long it would take them to die if they overshot the moon and went on into infinity.

All the same, when the count-down indicator began to flicker, his mind went blank in self-defence and he glued his eyes to it. Even Jimmy was showing signs of strain. There was a moment's delay after Jimmy pushed the firing button. The effect of the deceleration was almost instantaneous and they blacked out. When Hanson came round it was to hear the ground controller's voice, very faint now and far away,

"Orbit approach checked and correct. Good luck—out."

After that there was no time to speculate. What they had to do now had never been done before with such antiquated equipment. On previous moon landings the early pioneers had made a complete orbit of the moon before releasing the mooncraft. This was a luxury they could not afford. They had to get it right first time. For another thing, the mooncraft itself had never been tried out before. They had decided not to change into their up-to-date space-suits until they had gone into orbit. Now they regretted that decision. It took much longer than they had anticipated—they had not allowed enough for the effect that weightlessness would have on their movements. They scrambled into the mooncraft with minutes to spare and the last they saw of Jimmy was a cheery wave as he closed the airlock. They did not realize then that they were seeing him for the last time.

By the time they had strapped themselves in their seats they were exhausted by the sheer speed at which they had had to move during the last twenty minutes. Things had been happening so quickly that there had been no time to think. It was not the best preparation for what was to follow, but it gave them a chance to see Mashenko in action for the first time. It had been decided that since he was more experienced in precise calculations than the other two, he would take the controls for the last stage of the flight. Besides, although Hanson had not adduced it as a reason, he was the only one of the three to have had a full session on the hypnopaedic machine.

The operation was a delicate one. Since they could not risk making a complete circuit of the moon they had to start decelerating immediately from five thousand miles an hour to zero so as to come to a stop a few miles above their target, and they had to do it at a rate which would not cause them to black out. It involved using a combination of braking and vertical thrust rockets which demanded the most precise and delicate handling, as well as split-second timing. One small slip and they would be lost in the blackness of the lunar night.

Any doubts Hanson may have had about Mashenko vanished as soon as the big Russian took over the controls. Alone of the three, he seemed to be unaffected by the pressures that had built up during the last-minute rush. There was nothing in him now of the detached academic. His movements were precise and confident as if he were conducting a carefully planned experiment in his laboratory. He reached unerringly for the main switch and flicked it on. Then he firmly pulled the lever to disconnect them from the space-ship, waited a few measured seconds and fired the braking rockets. They were suddenly jolted forward into their seat-belts and the space-ship, which had been immediately above them, appeared momentarily in front as it shot away into the darkness.

Three quarters of an hour later Mashenko cut the braking rockets and the mooncraft swooped down behind the huge escarpment which towered above the south-west side of the reactor site. Once behind it, he fired the vertical thrust rockets and they floated slowly down to the surface. He turned to the others, a gleam of self-satisfaction in his eyes, "We've made it."

They scrambled out of the machine and Sarah, eager to test the stories she had heard about moon gravity, took a little jump which lifted her six feet above the ground.

Mashenko did his best to convey his disapproval of such unseemly frivolity—a difficult thing to do in a space-suit with nothing visible but your eyes, but somehow he succeeded.

Above them, against the starlight, they could see the jagged summit of the escarpment. Everything else was an unrelieved blackness. They switched on their helmet lamps and made their way over the rocky ground until they came to the point where the escarpment dropped sharply to the plain. There they stopped. They had almost an hour to wait before the work-day came to an end and they could move on the reactor control room.

While they waited Hanson told them about Blanchard. Up till now he had said nothing about his part in the affair because he could find no reasonable explanation for it. Mashenko was dubious. "You intend to find this man—now?"

"Yes, as soon as the convicts are shut in their quarters I'm going in there. I can use the service airlock."

"I think you are taking too big a risk—suppose the prisoners attack you?"

"Then I shall use this," and he patted his laser-gun. "He may be able to give us some help, and we are going to need all the help we can get."

Realizing from Hanson's tone that argument would be pointless, Mashenko said reluctantly, "Very well—I'll take you to the prison."

Once round the corner of the escarpment they were in full view of the reactor complex. It was unlikely that they would be seen since there were no windows in any of the buildings except the tunnelling and reactor control offices which faced away from them. All the same, they switched off their lamps and went hand in hand, Sarah in the middle. She was still not used to the effect of the low gravity and found difficulty in adjusting her strides to keep level with them. When they came out into the open they could see directly ahead of them the floodlights at the tunnel mouth and figures in white space-suits moving about. Half a mile to the left was the laboratory building, in darkness except for a shaft of light coming from the reactor control room window at the end facing the tunnel. The prison quarters were nowhere to be seen.

Mashenko said over the radio, "You must follow me round to the right until we can see it against the lights." Hand in hand they crossed the rocky surface in great bounds until Mashenko stopped and pointed. All they could see, silhouetted against the lights, was the sharp outline of what appeared to be a long semicircular building. They moved closer to it so that it screened them from the rest of the complex.

While they waited Mashenko went over again the normal routine of the site at the end of the work-day. After that they sat in silence, each preoccupied with his own thoughts, until Sarah jogged Hanson's arm and said, "Look—what's that?" She pointed to a row of lights approaching at high speed.

"That's the railcar—not long to wait now."

The lights came to a halt at the end of the laboratory building and presently another set of lights began moving out towards them and stopped at the end of the prison building. A few minutes later they started back towards the tunnel entrance.

Hanson said, "I'm going in now. You two wait here and if I am not out in quarter of an hour, come in after me."

Switching on his helmet lamp, he searched for the control button which opened the airlock. He found it and pushed. The outer door slid open and a blaze of light streamed out. Hanson cursed, slipped inside and closed the door. He called the other two on his suit radio. "If anyone saw that light they will come to investigate. Let me know if you see anyone coming." He was thankful that he had had the foresight to have their suit radios tuned to a frequency which would penetrate the thick cosmic ray shield which enveloped the building.

He passed through the equipment room and along a

narrow passage with a door at the other end. At the door he stopped and listened. Even through his helmet he could hear the sound of voices raised in argument. He hesitated a moment, then pushed it open.

Three convicts stood with their backs to him, doling out trays of food to the prisoners who were queueing behind a large counter in which the trays were stored. Two prisoners were fighting over a tray of food and the trusties behind the counter were shouting at them. One of the men in the queue called out, "Hell, who's that?"

As they turned to stare at him, Hanson pulled up his visor and brandished his laser-gun. "Don't move, any of you. This isn't a stun-ray—it can kill." He walked forward to the counter and a voice called out, "Hanson. How did you get here?"

Blanchard, bearded and almost unrecognizable, stepped out of the queue and came towards him.

"I've just dropped in, as you might say, but I don't think your friends are very glad to see me."

"They are a little bit sore, I'm afraid. They expected to be set free when Malib took over—in fact, they were promised just that if they agreed to co-operate—but nothing has changed. They work the same hours on the same food and are shut in here at the end of the day, just as before."

He turned to face the prisoners. "This man will not do you any harm. I can't promise that he will set you free, but if anything can be done for you, he is the man to do it. He is Deputy Chairman of Mooncom and his mother is Governor of Britain."

There was some muttering and shuffling of feet and somewhere in the background a voice said, "Don't make me laugh. It was his kind that sent us here in the first place—a bleeding matrician." There was some renewed muttering, then Hanson leapt on to the counter.

"I'm not in a position to promise you anything. Malib are in control of the moon and until we can get them out of the way I am almost as helpless as you are. All I can say is that if we are successful, the governments of the world will be grateful and I may be able to do something for you. What we need from you now is information, if you have it."

Blanchard said, "We don't know much—only what we have been able to piece together from odd remarks picked up on our space-suit radios. Come over here with me and I'll give you what we have."

He led him through the dining-hall and into the dormitory where he selected a two-tier bed and sat down on it. "This is mine. I haven't been here long enough to qualify for a top bunk."

Hanson said, "Look, I think explanations had better keep for the moment There are only three of us and we haven't much time."

Blanchard whistled. "Only three—you must be optimistic. Well, in that case I'll be brief. I don't know how many of them there are apart from the twenty-one convicts whom I assume you know about, but I think some of the warders may have gone over to them. At least two of them are still doing guard duties."

"How many guards do they have on here now?"

"Two in the reactor control room and they are changed every four hours with the shifts.

"Right. We're going to take them first, then catch the reliefs when they arrive. Are the controllers loyal or have they gone over to Malib?"

"Loyal, I imagine—otherwise why would they need guards?"

Hanson got up. "I'm going now. As soon as we have dealt with the guards I'll send Mashenko—he is a Russian physicist who works on the reactors and knows his way about here—over here with some space-suits. Then you can choose two convicts you can trust and bring them over to the reactor control room."

Blanchard nodded. "I think I can find two."

"Do you know who is behind this?"

"I'm afraid not—I didn't get near enough to them. I don't

think the convicts themselves knew."

Outside in the darkness Sarah and Mashenko were waiting. Sarah had freed the laser-gun in her holster and her hand was on the butt when the airlock opened. She relaxed when she recognized Hanson. He told them what he had learned and they made their way over to the laboratories, keeping clear of the light blazing from the control room windows.

When they got to the airlock in the centre of the building Mashenko said, "We must get one of them to come out. We can't risk using lasers in the control room. If we damage the equipment in there we might trigger off a nuclear explosion that would make a crater bigger than Copernicus."

Hanson thought for a moment. "One of us—it had better be you, Nikolai—must stand outside the window and sign to them to come out. That should bring one of them out, then Sarah and I can get him as he comes through the airlock."

Mashenko went off to the end of the building and the other two took up their positions, one on either side of the airlock. There was a delay of some minutes, then the outer door slid open and a tall space-suited figure stepped cautiously out, stun-ray at the ready. Hanson did not intend to kill him; he thought they would simply overpower him and deprive him of his weapon. But he had reckoned without Sarah. The laser beam caught the guard full in the chest. He staggered, clutched his chest with both hands, then tumbled to the ground. Sarah grinned through her visor.

"What now?" she asked.

"We'll wait for Nikolai. He's about the same size as this one—near enough to fool the other guard at first sight. He can take this stun-ray and knock him out."

Mashenko went in first, the dead guard's stun-ray in his hand. The other two followed a few paces behind. The door to the control room had been left open and they could see the four controllers sitting at their consoles behind a mass of dials and monitors. The other guard, a short, thick-set individual, was pacing the floor behind them. He turned when he heard Mashenko's footsteps. "What was . . ." Then he realized it was not his comrade. His hand dropped to the butt of his stun-ray, but before he could draw it Mashenko squeezed his trigger. There was a faint hum and the guard collapsed. The reactor controllers turned round and stared wide-eyed at the intruders. Sarah picked up the fallen guard's gun and kept them covered while Hanson removed his helmet.

"Who are you?"—this from a curly-headed young man who blinked as he spoke. Then recognition dawned in his eyes. "It's Mr Hanson, isn't it?—and Mr Mashenko. How did you get here, sir? We thought all the shuttles were being held here."

"We came the hard way—in an old-fashioned space rocket—a museum piece, in fact. Now that we are here we need your help. We need to know the set-up at the base. You had better start at the beginning and tell us what happened."

Mashenko turned to the oldest of the four, a grey-haired man in his fifties, and addressed him in Russian. The man replied rapidly in the same language, gesticulating energetically when he wanted to emphasize a point. When he had finished Mashenko translated for the benefit of the others.

The attack had come at the end of the work-day when the convicts were assembled in the tunnelling control building to hand in their space-suits. The warders, as Hanson had guessed, were totally unprepared for it. The whole thing had been carried out with the precision and timing of a well-planned manoeuvre on the football field. At a signal from one of the convicts each warder suddenly found himself between two footballers who promptly jumped on him. Two of them had their necks broken and two more were still in the sick bay. Two of the footballers then conducted the remaining convicts to their quarters with promises that they would be freed next day while the others went over to the laboratory building and locked up the entire day shift. Then all the infiltrators boarded the monorail car.

The people at the base were taken completely by surprise. The prisoners simply walked in, blasting away with the stun-rays taken from the warders. There was no resistance and it was all over in a matter of minutes.

Since then, for the majority of the staff, there had been little change in the routine of the base, apart from the presence of the guards and the fact that the International Commissioners were locked up under guard in their mess. The take-over had been announced over the loudspeakers and they had all been instructed to carry on working as normal.

At this point Hanson interrupted. "Who is their leader?"

The curly-headed young man who had spoken first piped up, "We don't know, sir—we've only heard his voice over the loudspeakers—a matrician voice it sounded like. Somebody saw a tall, fair-haired man who arrived the day it started, but no-one has seen him since." He paused, remembering something. "Oh—and there's another matrician, sir. He arrived the day before the convicts took over. He was waiting to go out to the asteroid belt and the chairman put him in your quarters. I think they are holding him prisoner there—at least I heard one of the guards complaining about having to take his meals over and saying he should be in the mess with the others."

That would be Hughes, Hanson guessed. His office had said that he had left on an inspection trip of some kind. He would be a useful ally if he could get to him.

But who was the fair-haired man? It was then that he remembered Fiona's remark about Lumsden having disappeared. Could he be the man? It was possible, he supposed. He recalled Lumsden's background—a man from a once-powerful family, destined to play a minor role for the rest of his life. He was the sort of material that revolutionary leaders are made from. Yes, it fitted in. Lumsden knew his movements the night he had been kidnapped and could have done it. Time would tell.

In the meantime there were other problems to be dealt with. The first thing to do was to get Sarah and Mashenko to collect three space-suits and then fetch Blanchard and his two chosen convicts back to the reactor control room.

When they had gone he asked the young controller, "Do the people at the base check with the guards during the shift?"

"No, sir, they don't bother. What could four of us do against two armed footballers?"

That at least was something. Their presence would not be discovered until the next shift arrived. After that they would have to start moving. The sensible thing would be to retain the element of surprise as long as possible and travel to the base in the railcar with the returning shift. Then, with four guards out of the way and some presumably asleep at the base, their task would be a little easier. He had ascertained from curly-head that there was always a guard on duty at the monorail airlock to check the returning shift. He would not be expecting them and should not be much of a problem. That would leave another seven footballers together with the two warders who had apparently gone over to Malib—still a formidable opposition.

It was nearly two hours before Sarah and Mashenko returned with Blanchard and his two men. They had had some difficulty with the space-suits. The first batch they brought would not fit—they had been chosen at random—and they had had to make a second visit to the tunnelling control building. Even so, the final results were not prepossessing. They looked an untidy, motley crew. Blanchard introduced them.

Keegan, a burly man of medium height with thick black wavy hair, was serving a life sentence for murder. He had killed a workmate in a quarrel over a game of cards. His righteous indignation had known no bounds when the judge refused to accept his plea in mitigation that the man had been cheating him consistently all evening. Murder was murder, she had said, no matter that the victim had been a rogue and a cheat, and sentenced him to moon-labour for life. He felt somehow that he had been unjustly treated and now he was ready to have a crack at anyone to avenge himself on society. He had already severely beaten up three of his fellow convicts for imagined slights.

Deacon, the other one was a small weasel-faced individual. He had been sentenced to five years for beating his wife and, like Keegan, he had a grudge against society. He had a cunning, vicious look which more than made up for his light build.

Hanson explained his plan to Blanchard and said, "I want you to stay here with your friends and hold it if anything goes wrong. You will have four stun-rays between you and that should allow you deal with any attack coming through an airlock. These guns have a fairly wide arc of fire and four of them fired simultaneously should knock out everyone inside. Unless you get a call from us beforehand you should assume that anyone arriving by monorail is hostile. I suggest you post one man in the security room. There are indicator lamps there which light up when the outer door of either airlock is opened. If you are quick you will just have time to get there before the inner doors open. One more thing—we better have a code word, say elephants. If I call you and make no mention of elephants you will know that I have been captured and am making the call under duress."

Blanchard nodded, "I think we can cope."

While the others dragged the dead guard and the stunned one into a store room and locked them up, Hanson proceeded to get Blanchard's story. Before coming away from the prison quarters he had managed to shave himself and now looked more like the well-educated and highly intelligent matrician. He glanced at the clock which showed nearly an hour to go before the relief shift would arrive. "It's rather a long story, but you have some time in hand, so I may as well start at the beginning.

"For a long time now I have thought that matrician society had become too rigid and that sooner or later it is going to break down unless we do something about it. Everyone has a fixed place in our world and knows that he is going to remain in it for the whole of his life. With minor limitations imposed by ability, every man can predict what his career will be and where he will finish up. It is the same for all classes. You and I are just as much bound by it as a Delta clerk or an Epsilon labourer.

"The human race has evolved through a process of continuous change and will only continue to survive if it goes on developing. All ruling classes—and ours is no exception—tend to maintain the *status quo* in order to stay in power. By resisting change of any kind they bottle up the natural forces of change until they explode. The explosion is followed by a period of more or less uncontrolled violence until a new social pattern emerges.

"I began looking for weak points in the fabric of our society to see if I could predict where we would be vulnerable, and came to the conclusion that the moon was the key. Whoever controlled it could virtually control the world. What I could not see was how, with our system of checks and balances, any one group could achieve this.

"I knew about the Malib messages in computer print-outs, of course, but, like everyone else, I was inclined to pooh-pooh them. I could not see how they could possibly bring it off.

"What happened next was almost sheer accident. I had dropped the idea of some sort of revolution and was looking for more subtle signs that might indicate long-term decay in our social fabric. Then, one day when I was bored, I happened to be going through the monthly traffic figures and noticed that the number of convicts going to the moon was rather higher than I had remembered. Normally I was only interested in the overall figure but that day, as I said, I was bored and decided to look at it more closely. I discovered that the two previous months' convictions had also been higher than usual. Then, out of curiosity, I got someone to dig out the conviction records for me. What I found . . ."

Hanson interrupted, "Yes, I know about that. What happened next?"

"I began to wonder if there was any connection between these convictions and the Malib messages—those Gamma-class convictions, I mean, which did not arise from Malib meetings. There was only one way to find out—to talk to the wives of the convicted men. The first three I spoke to refused to discuss it and this seemed natural enough—they were ashamed and didn't want to talk about it. I tried a few more and got the same result. By then I was convinced I was on to something. It didn't seem reasonable that there should not be a single wife who would talk.

"Then I got what seemed to be my first break. A footballer's wife called me at my flat one evening and said that she had heard I wanted to talk to someone whose husband had been sent to the moon—a friend, another footballer's wife, had told her. She suggested that I come to her flat the following evening.

"Before I left the office next day I left a message for you with one of the clerks—did you get it?"

Hanson nodded and Blanchard went on, "I don't know why I left the message—must have been a premonition of some kind. Anyway, I turned up at her flat at the appointed time and she led me into the living module. She offered me some coffee and I sat down to wait while she fetched it. She came out after a few moments, but without the coffee. She ripped her dress down the front and called out, "He's here. Come and get him." Two men, both of them Gammas, rushed out of the sleeping module and grabbed me. One of them held me down while the other went over to the woman, ripped her underwear off, hit her a few times and then got on top of her—all this with her co-operation.

"When he had finished, one of them called the police and

the woman scratched my face and tore at my tunic. You can imagine how it felt—pinned down there watching the evidence being fabricated before my eyes. There was nothing I could do about it. Two days later I came up before the tribunal and was sentenced to death. As you know, in rape cases the onus of proof is on the accused. The medical evidence alone was enough to have convicted me without the additional evidence of the two men who 'happened to have called on her' at the right moment. I would have been executed that afternoon if it weren't for the fact that, since I was a matrician, the sentence had to be ratified by your mother."

Blanchard grinned ruefully. "It was not an experience I'd care to repeat. It was about four hours before the reprieve came through—the longest four hours of my life. Next morning I was on my way here. I saw you in the transit satellite but you didn't notice me."

Hanson nodded. "Yes, I was told that one of the convicts had looked at me as if he knew me, but you had gone when I turned round."

Mashenko came over to where they were sitting. "We have a problem. When the new shift arrives they assemble in the airlock and one of the relief guards comes along here to check that everything is okay. Then he goes back and the new shift comes in with the two guards behind them. We can't risk shooting into the airlock—we might kill the controllers."

Sarah, who had been listening to Blanchard's story, cut in, "We must find a way of drawing the second guard—I know. Suppose we do something to make the first man call out. The other, if he has any sense, will shut the controllers in the airlock and come out himself. Then one of us could take him as he comes out. How does that sound?"

Hanson considered this and said, "I see nothing wrong with that—provided we can make the first guard call out loudly enough."

Sarah's features broke into a smile of gleeful anticipation.

"I think I can guarantee that."

The airlock which served the monorail was at the far end of the building from the control room. When the railcar docked the outer door opened automatically and lit the warning lamps over the inner door and in the security room. After a ten-second delay the inner door opened.

The corridor leading from the airlock was a narrow one, only just wide enough to take two people walking abreast, and turned at right angles before reaching the security room. Sarah took up her position there with the door open and kept her eyes on the warning lamp.

Adjacent to the airlock was a small store room used for maintenance materials and into this Hanson and Mashenko squeezed themselves with inches to spare. When the warning lamp came on they shut the door and waited. There was a barely audible hiss as the inner door of the airlock slid open and then the guard's footsteps echoed along the corridor. The footsteps died away and they tensed themselves, scarcely daring to breathe. For a moment there was silence and then a shriek of agony rent the air. Sarah had kept her promise.

A few seconds later they heard the airlock close and the second guard running past their hiding-place. Hanson opened the door, took careful aim and fired. The thin pencil of blue light caught the guard in the back of the head. He tottered a few steps, stone dead, and then crashed to the floor. Hanson raced down the corridor—there was just a chance that the scream they had heard had not come from the guard. He rounded the corner in time to see Sarah calmly and deliberately fire her laser into the head of the guard who was writhing on the floor.

"What on earth made him scream like that?"

For answer, Sarah bent down and turned the body over. In the centre of his trouser fly was a tiny charred hole, still smouldering.

Ten minutes later they were sitting in the railcar, hurtling silently through the lunar night at two hundred and fifty miles an hour. The four reactor controllers, by now thoroughly frightened, were huddled together in the forward end of the car. From time to time they cast nervous glances at the three behind them.

Hanson reviewed their position. So far they had been lucky, but the difficult part of the operation lay ahead of them. There would be nine guards to deal with including the two renegade warders as well as the seven other convicts. Then there was Lumsden, if in fact it was he, and any of the regular staff who may have defected. It was unlikely that any of them had gone over to Malib—they had all been carefully screened before being appointed to the moon—but he couldn't afford to count on it.

On the credit side there was an advantage he had not bargained for. He had learned from the reactor controllers that the Malib group wore their space suits all the time except, presumably, when they were asleep. The other suits in the base were kept locked up and issued only when needed. They should have no difficulty in identifying the enemy and, with any luck, since they were wearing identical space suits, they would have a few moments' grace before they were recognized as intruders.

He signed to the other two to come back out of earshot of the controllers and outlined his plan for the next stage.

"When we arrive at the base we must leave the car first and you, Sarah, will deal with the guard who will be waiting in the vestibule. There are two corridors running out from the vestibule. The one on the right leads to the main part of the building; the other one leads directly to the commissioners' quarters where my rooms are. As far as we know they are holding Hughes there and not using them for anything else. We can make them our base.

"One of us will have to remain by the airlock to deal with anyone coming to look for the guard when he doesn't show up. That had better be you, Nikolai, since Sarah does not know her way about so well. As soon as you have dealt with whoever shows up you can join us. We should, with any luck, be able to get there without being seen. By this time most people will either be in bed or in the recreation areas."

"What then?" Sarah asked. "What's the next move?"

Hanson smiled. There was something infectious about her eagerness which, although he would probably not have admitted it, even to himself, gave a badly needed boost to his confidence. She, alone of the three, was enjoying every minute of it.

"This is where being deputy chairman comes in handy. My office is in my rooms and I have a monitor screen which covers all the vital parts of the building. We can see what is going on and make our plans accordingly."

Suddenly brilliant sunshine poured in through the observation ports. Sarah sat up startled. "What . . ."

Hanson laughed. "I had forgotten you didn't know. We have moved into the daylight zone where there will be nothing but sunshine for another week. Come to the other side and I'll show you. There were mountains on either side and, looking through the port, they could see the line of pylons supporting the monorail curving away behind them into utter darkness. This had been a part of his daily life for so long now that he scarcely noticed it, but now he took delight in explaining it to Sarah to whom it was all new and exciting.

As they came out from between the mountains with their fantastic patterns of sharply divided light and shadow, the railcar began gradually to lose speed. "What's that?" Sarah asked, pointing to a huge cylindrical structure stretching out across the plain. Near it a gigantic mechanical excavator was scooping up rocks and dust from the surface.

"That's part of our mining operation—the surface rocks here are full of various minerals. The long cylindrical thing is a Mass Accelerator. The excavator scoops up the surface and pours it into these large buckets which you can see. The buckets are accelerated through the coils and when they reach the end, the contents are launched into space and travel slowly to the Alpha Satellites where they are fed into solar-powered furnaces and the minerals extracted. The buckets travel back to this end of the accelerator to be used again."

Now they could see the moonbase ahead of them, a gleaming white hemisphere, dazzling in the glaring sunlight. They closed their visors and moved to the front of the car.

Sarah stepped out from the airlock. The guard, who was leaning casually against the wall, gave her an idle glance and then his eyes opened wide with surprise and alarm. He was still wearing a surprised expression when they dragged his body into the airlock. The four reactor controllers stared at him, incredulity written all over their features, and hurried off towards the main part of the building. They had been instructed to behave as if nothing had happened, but Hanson doubted whether they could carry it off. It had been, he supposed, a nerve-shattering experience for them and it showed in their faces.

Hanson and Sarah strolled casually into the left-hand corridor leading to the commissioners' quarters, but their casualness was more apparent than real. The corridor was empty and they continued their stroll until they came to the door of Hanson's quarters. He pulled out his magnetic key and inserted it in the slot in the door jamb. The door slid open noiselessly and they slipped inside the small hallway which served as an anteroom to the office section of the rooms. The door to the office was open and they could hear voices raised in anger. Hanson motioned Sarah to silence and moved cautiously towards the doorway, thanking Providence in the shape of the world government which had seen fit to furnish the commissioners' quarters with the most luxurious of thick carpets. He opened his visor so as to hear better. Lumsden's voice came over clearly, "I've had enough of your damned arrogance, Hughes. I'm going to settle your . . ." At that moment Hanson burst into the room.

The two men were facing each other and Lumsden, wearing a space-suit but without the helmet, was brandishing a stun-ray. He spun round. "What the . . ." and then the laser beam scorched his temple.

Hughes stood gaping, too surprised to say anything and looking as startled as Lumsden had. Hanson removed his helmet.

"Well, of all the . . . Hanson! . . . thank God . . . that lunatic was going to kill me." He mopped his brow with his hand and sat down heavily behind the desk. Sarah had come in by now and he looked from one to the other in what seemed like consternation. He mopped his brow again. "Sorry . . . a moment ago I was as good as dead . . . then you appeared and . . . how did you get here? . . . I thought . . ."

"Relax—we're not ghosts," Hanson grinned, "even though we did come out of the past, as it were. We found a carefully preserved antique at Cape Kennedy and managed to get it here—only just in time by the look of things. By the way, let me introduce . . . First Officer Wilson from the Game Park—Mr Hughes."

"Are there any more of you?"

"Only one. He is attending to one of the guards. He'll be along presently."

A thought struck Hanson, "You said Lumsden was about to kill you—with a stun-ray?"

"Yes, it has been modified. I don't really understand these things, but apparently it has been fitted with an amplifier to increase its power. He killed one of the prison warders with it."

Hanson set his laser down on the desk and picked up the stun-ray. He pointed it at a picture hanging on the wall and pulled the trigger. The frame and the glass disintegrated, leaving only the canvas hanging. They felt the shock wave bouncing back from the wall.

"I hope there aren't any more like this."

"I can't help you there, I'm afraid. Tell me, where did

you make your landing?"

"At the reactors—we killed the guards and came here on the monorail." Hughes had recovered his composure by now and got up from the desk.

"What are you going to do now?"

"We'll wait here until Mashenko has dealt with whoever goes to look for the guard on the airlock. Then we can use the monitors to see where the rest of the guards are. We should be able to take them one at a time. In fact, I'll have a look now to see how Mashenko is getting on."

Hanson walked round the desk to get at the monitor controls. He sat down and glanced idly at a sheet of paper lying on the desk. It was a list of names with biographical details. Remarks had been written in the margin against some of them. He was puzzled for a moment, then the penny dropped. These must be the suggested names for provisional governments which Malib had asked for. Hughes was too quick for him. He grabbed Hanson's laser from the desk and sprang back to cover both of them.

"Don't move, either of you."

Hanson glanced at Sarah. Her gun was still in its holster. He sought for some way to attract Hughes's attention to himself.

"So it was you, after all, you little bastard. I might have known Lumsden couldn't do this on his own."

Hughes glared at him and made a gesture with the laser. "I'll . . ."

Sarah launched herself silently at him, but she was too late. Hughes fired without turning his head and the laser beam caught her full in the chest. She crashed to the floor, face down, and lay still.

"That was clever, Hanson, but not quite clever enough. Get away from that desk and stand over there against the wall." Keeping Hanson covered, he punched out a number on the visiphone.

Mashenko listened to the footsteps of the others die away

down the corridor and settled down to wait. For the first time since they landed he felt confident. So far everything had gone like clockwork. True, they had been lucky as far as the landing was concerned, but the rest of the operation had gone according to plan without a single hitch. Once they were established in Hanson's office they could plan the next stage. It should not be difficult with the monitor to help them. He was surprised at his own coolness; even the body of the dead guard did not disturb him although he was pressed up hard against it in an effort to conceal them both from anyone approaching down the corridor from the main part of the building.

For all his new-found confidence he had not yet formed any clear plan of action to deal with the next arrival. Perhaps it was that he had not yet accepted the idea of having to kill. He had the dead guard's stun-ray—he could use that.

It was a long time before he heard footsteps coming from the main area of the building. He listened to them carefully; there seemed to be only one person approaching. He braced himself against the wall and eased off the safety catch. The footsteps came nearer, then stopped. He could not judge how far away they were. After a moment they advanced again.

He stepped out into the vestibule, caught a glimpse of a figure in a white space-suit and fired in its general direction. It collapsed and the stun-ray it had been carrying clattered across the floor. Quickly he dragged the unconscious guard into the airlock and closed it. Then, picking up the abandoned stun-ray, he made his way along the corridor towards Hanson's quarters.

Hanson stood with his back to the wall, tasting the bitterness of defeat. There was nothing he could do to warn Mashenko; he would walk straight into the guard summoned by Hughes. His helmet with its tiny built-in radio was lying on the table several yards away. Hughes walked over to Sarah and, keeping his laser trained on Hanson, turned her body over with his foot. She was dead. Her sightless eyes stared up at the ceiling.

Anger welled up inside Hanson. Sarah's death had been all his fault. If only he had . . . There was no use thinking about it now. Nothing could bring her back; she would never have the child she had wanted. It was then that he made up his mind to kill Hughes. It no longer mattered that Malib had won and would take over the world. That seemed irrelevant now. If Hughes allowed him to live long enough he would find a way to kill him, even at the cost of his own life if necessary.

It was almost as if Hughes had read his mind. "You can relax, Hanson—I'm not going to kill you—not yet at least. I've got the world by the shorts now, but it will do no harm to have a hostage. Besides, I might even persuade you to join me."

Hanson said nothing, but looked coldly at his captor. Hughes went on, "In fact, I have to thank you for ridding me of that oaf Lumsden, I had intended to dispose of him anyway, but, until you arrived so opportunely, it looked rather as if the boot was on the other foot."

In spite of his anger Hanson was curious. "Why did you want to kill your own man?"

"Lumsden was dangerous and I had no further use for him. He was a bungler—dropping you in the Game Park instead of killing you. There were other things too—he had a chip on his shoulder—felt he was not getting the recognition his qualities deserved." Hughes paused, as if a new idea had come to him. "Now you—that would be a different proposition. You are a man of ability like myself, wasting your talents on a hum-drum job an intelligent child could do. If you were to join me there would be nothing we could not achieve. Think of it, man—the whole world as a plaything to mould the way we want it, and all those other worlds out there that we haven't touched yet."

"Might not your colleagues have something to say about

that?"

"Colleagues?—I have none. Malib doesn't exist; it is a figment of the imagination."

"But . . ."

"Malib was nothing more than messages inserted in computer print-outs and a few dozen Gammas programmed to believe in it." Hughes's eyes glowed with self-satisfied triumph. "It was really quite easy. You see, my last appointment was in the education department—I was responsible for Gamma educational programmes. It was not very difficult, once I had found suitable subjects, to insert passages about Malib in their hypnopaedic programmes. They came to believe that Malib was a vast organization with branches in every country and that they were a part of it. Once they had been conditioned to believe that—it took about a year before I was sure of them—I fed them detailed instructions about the parts they were to play. That was slightly more difficult because I had to make sure that truth drugs would not get it out of them. I experimented on some of them with doses of Veritin. In the end I gave each a trigger sentence and programmed them so that their minds would remain a complete blank on the subject until the trigger sentence was used."

"But suppose someone accidentally used one of these sentences?"

"That would be most improbable," Hughes smiled. "What interrogator would be likely to say, 'Crocodiles eat blue potatoes' or 'Elephants can only fly slowly?'

"The computer messages were easy, of course. Computer programming is one of the standard Gamma educational courses."

Hanson could not but admire the man. It was no wonder that the security people had got nowhere in their investigations—finding something that doesn't exist is not the easiest of tasks. Hughes was quick to notice that he had impressed his hearer.

"You know, you might do worse than join me. Between

us, you and I could save humanity from death by stagnation. What the world needs is a challenge and that is precisely what the women will not let us have. Every new development or line of research is debated by committees, sometimes for years, and in the end nine out of ten are shelved because they might lead us into situations we are not equipped to handle. We never will be equipped unless we accept the challenge and the risks.

"They began by banning genetic engineering and they have extended it to cover every field of human activity. By now we ought to be half way across the galaxy instead of piddling about in the asteroid belt, digging up minerals."

Hughes was interrupted by two guards who charged into the room. They had obviously been asleep from their appearance. The sight of the two bodies on the floor brought them up short and they stared in amazement at them. "Don't stand there gawping," Hughes said acidly. "We've been attacked. There's a man in a space-suit coming in from the monorail airlock—get him as he comes in, but don't use your stun-rays—you'll only have to carry him if you knock him out. I'll keep an eye on this one."

Mashenko didn't have a chance. He walked unsuspecting through the open door and the guards pounced on him. His hands were laden with the stun-rays he had taken from the guards at the airlock and before he could get them free he was seized in an iron grip and frog-marched into the office. The bewildered expression on his face was almost comic, but Hanson was in no mood for comedy. He had brought them here, Sarah and Mashenko, and he had failed them. Sarah was dead and Mashenko looked like going the same way.

"Who is this man?" Hughes asked, turning to Hanson.

"Nikolai Mashenko."

"Mashenko? I've heard that name somewhere . . . I know, the Venusium man. Another good catch. We really are having quite a day."

"Let him go," he ordered the guards. "Let's have them

out of those space-suits first. I'm not taking any chances with this pair."

Mashenko stood watching Hughes, but made no move to comply.

"Come on," Hughes snarled. "Do you want me to burn a little hole in you?" and he aimed the laser at the Russian's feet.

When they had divested themselves of their space-suits Hughes ordered the guards. "Take them along to one of the spare rooms in this corridor and lock them in. I don't want them in with the others. I want these two checked twice an hour at random intervals. When you've done that come back here and get rid of these bodies."

As they left, Hanson took a last look at Sarah who, only minutes ago, had been so full of life.

The rooms selected for them by the guards were those of the Junior African Commissioner and were furnished on a more modest scale than Hanson's. They were, in fact, the rooms which Hanson had occupied himself when he had been a junior commissioner several years previously. There was no office—that was a privilege reserved for the chairman and deputy chairman. Next down the scale were the senior commissioners who did not have their own dining-rooms but were allowed to have breakfast in their quarters. Last of all came the junior commissioners who ate all their meals in the mess and who were provided only with a sitting-room, bedroom and bathroom.

When the guards had gone and locked the door, Mashenko asked, "What happened?" Hanson explained, making it quite clear that he blamed himself for the débâcle.

"We've still got Blanchard—I wonder if we can get in touch with him." Hanson went over to the visiphone and keyed the number of the reactor control room. The screen remained blank. He tried some other numbers in the base itself but the result was the same.

"They're not taking any chances. You know what this

means?" Mashenko shook his head. "Neither Hughes nor Lumsden would have the detailed knowledge necessary to switch individual instruments out of the circuit. One of the base maintenance staff must have done this for them. That means we can't count on any help from inside. We don't know how many may have gone over to Hughes. Poor old Blanchard—he won't have a chance."

He began to pace about the room. There had to be some way out—he couldn't accept that all this effort and loss of life had been to no purpose. He owed it to Sarah, if not to the others, to do something about it. He went to the bathroom, poured himself a glass of water and came back with it. As he sat down to drink it something jabbed him in the groin. For a moment it didn't register. Then he jumped to his feet and Mashenko watched in amazement as he zipped open his trouser fly and groped around inside.

"It's all right—I haven't gone crazy yet—look at this," and he fished out the laser. "This is a small laser—we must be able to do something with it. Let's sit down and think it over. We're not finished yet, but this may be our last chance and we don't want to muff it." He slipped the laser into his trouser pocket and sat down again.

Blanchard woke with a start . . . he must have dozed off. The two convicts were stretched on the floor, their bodies contorted in the unattractive postures of sleep. The reactor controllers were seated at their consoles, talking in low tones and pausing occasionally to scan their monitors. It was this low hum of conversation that had lulled him to sleep. He glanced at the clock. It was now almost three hours since Hanson and the others had left and there had been no word from them. Something must have gone wrong. By now the monorail car bringing the relief shift would be getting ready to leave. If they had failed and been caught, guards would be sent to the laboratory to make sure there were no more of them. He considered his sleeping companions; they would be helpless against trained men who were expecting opposition. Their only chance was to get away before the railcar arrived. They would have to use the emergency hydrojet.

He knew from his time in Space Transport that there were two of them, one at each monorail terminal, to be used in the event of an accident or breakdown. He rubbed his eyes and struggled to his feet.

"Where is the emergency hydrojet kept?" One of the controllers replied, "It is usually parked in a hangar next to Tunnelling Control." Blanchard shook Keegan who dragged himself to his feet grumbling and protesting. "Come on, we're going to the base. Wake Deacon and get your helmets on."

He turned to the controllers. "It looks as if our friends have run into problems. I'm not going to ask you to stick your necks out for our sake, but when the guards arrive I would be grateful if you told them I was on my own. They are not likely to go to the prison quarters and count the convicts. Will you do that?"

They were not very happy about it but eventually they agreed to do as he asked and he set off with Keegan and Deacon for the hangar.

It was almost half an hour later when they climbed into the emergency hydrojet. Blanchard thanked the streak of conscientiousness that had impelled him to familiarize himself with every type of transport his office had to deal with. He had never actually flown one of the hydrojets adapted for use on the moon, but he understood the controls. These craft had no rudders but they were fitted with vertical and lateral jets which allowed them to land almost anywhere on the moon's surface and gave them a speed of about six hundred miles an hour.

His passengers were a little nervous. Neither of them had been off the ground in any sort of craft except for their passage to the moon. When he pulled the main switch and fired the vertical jets their nervousness was not allayed. The plane leapt upwards, jarring every bone in their bodies.

Blanchard grinned at them. "Sorry, I haven't flown one of these before." He checked their ascent and cautiously opened the lateral jets a fraction. This time he had got it right and the hydrojet began to move slowly forwards. He switched on the nose and belly lights and, with careful adjustments to the throttles, succeeded in bringing the machine over the laboratory building. From there they would have to use the monorail track to navigate by. It was not easy, especially when the track curved and they lost it momentarily. Then they had to weave about in the darkness until they picked up the thin line reflected in their lights. After about quarter of an hour the lights of the railcar flashed past below them, travelling in the opposite direction.

Mashenko emerged from the bathroom with a glass of water in his hand. "Tell me," he asked, "why are the ventilation grilles set so low in the bathroom wall? Everywhere else in the building they are almost at ceiling height."

Hanson suppressed a momentary irritation at having his train of thought interrupted. "I don't know . . . never really thought about it. My God—yes, I do know. Listen, when this building was designed they made provision for the commissioners to have their meals in their quarters—the sort of system we have in London. By the time they had decided we should eat in the mess this section was already finished and it was easier to leave the service duct in place—and it's big enough for a man to get through."

He got to his feet and started pacing about the room. "I've got it. If we can cut into the duct we can crawl through it to the chairman's quarters. Lumsden was using them, so they should be empty now. It has monitors like mine—and an extra one I only learned about last month when they told me I was to be the next chairman—it monitors my office." He slapped his hand on the table. "And—there's something else—a manual override on every essential system in the building."

Mashenko, overcome by the torrent of words, stared at him in bewilderment. This excited character was not the Hanson he had come to know, not the cool imperturbable administrator.

"If that is so, won't Hughes move in there?"

"No. Unless the chairman told him about it, there is no way he could find out. The controls are in a secret panel on the underside of the desk. Krishna Narayan is a wily old bird—he would not have revealed it. As far as Hughes knows, the chairman's office is an exact duplicate of mine."

There was, he reflected, only one snag. By the time he had cut his way into the duct and out again into the chairman's office, the laser would be useless as a weapon. The tiny battery which powered it would be exhausted. Once the guards discovered their absence it would only be a matter of time before they were found again—and not much time at that. The guards—that was it—why hadn't he thought of it before? They would not send two guards to check on them—one would be enough. He could start cutting into the duct now and then wait until after the first check had been made. With luck that would leave him a clear half hour before the next check. If Mashenko could somehow knock out the next guard he could take his stun-ray and bring it to the chairman's quarters.

The entrance to the junior commissioner's rooms was a short passage containing only a built-in cupboard for storing a space-suit. It opened into the sitting-room from which another short passage led at right angles to the bathroom and bedroom. If the guard should turn up while Hanson was cutting into the duct there would be time for Mashenko to warn him.

Shut in the tiny bathroom, Hanson set to work. He selected a point about three feet above where the waste pipes entered the wall. Fortunately the steel of the inner wall was thin and would not take much power to cut.

By the time he had cut a slit about six inches long the

room was filled with acrid smoke. He came out and closed the door behind him. The fumes could be smelt quite clearly in the passage. He looked at his watch; the guard might arrive within ten minutes. When he went into the bathroom again he found that the fumes had disappeared. He cut another slit and repeated the performance until there was only one cut left to make.

No sooner had he gone in to make the last cut than he heard a glass smash on the floor—Mashenko's warning signal. Quickly he closed the door and returned to the sitting-room. The guard was standing in the doorway regarding him suspiciously, stun-ray pointed at him. He said nothing but his eyes travelled slowly round the room and back again to Hanson. Motioning them aside with his gun, he walked over to the other passage. Hanson held his breath. To go into the passage would have meant turning his back on his prisoners, so the guard contented himself with a quick glance along it, Satisfied, he crossed the room, keeping them covered, and did not turn his back until he was at the outer door.

Hanson moved quickly into the bathroom and cut away the last section of steel. He crawled inside the duct and slowly felt his way along it, counting the waste pipe outlets as he went. When he came to the fifth one he stopped, put his ear against the wall and listened.

There was no sound from the other side of the wall. He switched on the laser and began to cut. Provision for air circulation in the main duct was minimal and in no time at all it was filled with the acrid fumes of burning paint and white hot steel. Half choked and eyes streaming, he made another quick cut at right angles to the first and forced outwards the resultant triangular piece of steel. This allowed some of the fumes to escape into the bathroom and he went on cutting blindly. Instead of a neat rectangle, the finished cut-out looked like a piece of a jig-saw puzzle.

He lurched through the bathroom and out into the corridor, gasping for air. When he had recovered his breath and cleared his streaming eyes he went through to the office section of the rooms and switched on the lights.

First he had to check the override panel which he had heard about but not actually seen. He ran his hand along the underside of the desk until he felt the circular rough patch which indicated the release catch. The panel slid out and he sat down to study it. There were override controls for every air-tight door in the building, including the external airlocks, so that, in the event of a fire or damaged air seal, any part of the building could be isolated. There was similar provision for isolating the power circuits in each area. He could seal off and immobilize any part of the base at will.

Next he switched on the monitor screen and tuned it to his own office. Hughes was alone and appeared to be watching his monitor which was outside the range of the scanner. Hanson switched in the close-up device and examined the monitor control panel in front of Hughes, looking for the depressed button which would show what area was being screened. It was airlock number three and he switched his own screen to that. It showed two guards, stun-rays in their hands, standing one on either side of the airlock. This puzzled him. Why should Hughes have guards there? Curious, he tuned into the other two airlocks. The monorail terminal was unguarded, but there were two guards on airlock number two. Clearly they were expecting an attack.

It could only be Blanchard. Hanson looked at his watch—by now the relief shift would have arrived at the reactor complex and discovered what had happened. Blanchard must have taken the emergency hydrojet and got out before they arrived.

Hanson switched on the emergency transceiver which shared a special frequency with the emergency craft, but it was dead. It would not have occurred to Blanchard to switch on his transceiver. There was no way he could warn him of the reception committee awaiting him and no way of telling which airlock he would try to use.

He thought quickly then turned to the override panel and locked the inner doors of both airlocks. Then he checked the monorail monitor. It showed the railcar about one third of the way to the base. He cut its power supply. If there were any guards on board that would help to even the odds.

Alone in the junior commissioner's rooms, Mashenko was worried. He had hoped to conceal himself in the space-suit storage cupboard and take the guard from behind as he went towards the sitting-room, but it was too small. There was no way he could squeeze his vask bulk into it. It was almost half an hour since the last check and the guard could appear any minute now. He had to think of something quickly—and it had to be foolproof. There would be no second chance.

It was some minutes before he realized that the room was stuffed with weapons—at first he had thought of them only as decorations. The junior African commissioner had decorated the walls of the sitting-room with relics from his country's far distant past—grotesquely carved heads, shields made from animal skins, clubs and spears that must have represented a small fortune with antique prices as they were.

Mashenko picked up a club but rejected it. The heavy wood would make little impression on a space helmet if the guard was wearing one. Next he selected an ancient spear from the wall and examined it. The blade, although eaten away in places was still sharp, but would it cut through the double skin of tear-resistant material from which space-suits were made?

He had no time to make up his mind. As he stood pondering the spear he heard the door slide open and the guard's heavy footstep. He moved quickly to one side of the entrance and stood against the wall, spear poised at shoulder height. The guard, seeing no-one from the entrance, advanced slowly into the room, holding his stun-ray out in front of him. As the muzzle of the gun appeared Mashenko tensed himself, then lunged forward with all the strength he could muster. The guard staggered and dropped his gun. Mashenko dived for it, picked it up and fired while the guard was still on his feet, contemplating with a stupefied expression the spear which was protruding from his ribs.

He forced his way into the duct with some difficulty—he was a bigger man than Hanson—and crawled uncomfortably along it. Hanson had thoughtfully switched on the bathroom light so that he had no trouble finding the exit hole.

Blanchard, still dazzled by the glaring sunlight, eased back on the lateral jets and brought the emergency craft round in a wide sweep to circle the building. During his time at Space Transport he had made several visits to the moon, but his memory of the layout was hazy. He made a complete circuit of the building and settled on the airlock nearest to where the satellite shuttle was parked. That was the entrance he had used before. He was still a little clumsy with the controls and overshot it at the first attempt and had to make another circuit. The second time he was successful and set the hydrojet down gently a few yards from the outer door of the airlock.

They scrambled out of the machine and made for the door. Not for the first time Blanchard found himself wondering if he had made the right choice of companions. Keegan, aggressive and hot-tempered would give a good account of himself, but might be rash. Deacon he was not so sure about. He was a cunning little man and, like Keegan, he had a grudge against society, but he was a bully and probably not over-endowed with physical courage.

He found the switch for the outer door and pushed it. The door slid open and they went inside, closing it after them. Blanchard said, "By now the guards at the laboratory will have alerted them, but they will only be expecting one man on his own. Deacon and I will stand one at each side of the door and you, Keegan, in the centre. As soon as it opens, keep firing straight out into the passage."

When they were in position he took a deep breath and pushed the switch. Nothing happened. He pushed it again, once . . . twice . . . three times . . . and still nothing happened. "This one must be out of order—we'll have to try the other one."

They left the hydrojet where it was and made their way on foot round the outside of the dome until they came to the second airlock. Alongside it was a ladder with rungs running up to the base of the antenna array on the peak of the dome. This must be the maintenance exit. As far as Blanchard remembered, it opened into a narrow passage at the other end of which was an air-tight door leading to the stores and workshop area. They went in and, once again, Blanchard pushed the outer door switch.

Hanson looked up when Mashenko entered the room. "Blanchard is on his way here and there are guards on both airlocks. I have closed them off for the moment so that the inner doors can't be opened. As soon as we see which door Blanchard tries first you can make for the other one and take the guards from behind. Then I'll release the door and you can bring Blanchard and his convicts back here. Take two towels from the bathroom and wrap them round your boots to muffle the sound."

They waited, watching the monitor panel. When the lamp lit to indicate that the outer door of the main airlock had been opened, Hanson said, "Now. As fast as you can to the maintenance airlock—good luck."

When he had gone Hanson continued watching the main airlock. The two guards were looking in a puzzled fashion at the door which showed no sign of opening although the outer door had been closed again. The lamp came on and, a few seconds later went off again to indicate that someone had opened the outer door and then closed it. The guards appeared to be holding a conference. After a moment one of them started back along the corridor to the main part of the building. Hanson dashed to the override panel—he had almost forgotten the system of air-tight doors that could be used to seal off each section of the building. Quickly he scanned the panel until he found the buttons he was looking for. He pressed them and the doors closed, shutting off the airlock from the rest of the building. He watched the guards rushing from one door to the other and grinned to himself, then switched the monitor to his own office. Hughes had evidently been watching the scene at the airlock, to judge from the expression of puzzled consternation on his face. As Hanson watched, he switched his monitor screen over and then, after a moment's pause, called someone on the visiphone.

Hanson switched his screen to the maintenance airlock in time to see the two guards crumple to the floor. Mashenko had evidently arrived. He used the override panel to release the inner door of the airlock and then returned to the monitor panel to find out what Hughes had been up to. Systematically he examined every part of the building covered by the scanners. What he saw appalled him.

In the main recreation room there were eleven men wearing space-suits, some armed with stun-rays and others carrying small metallic objects which he could not identify. He made a quick count. Assuming there were two guards at the reactor complex, that meant that Hughes had deployed his whole force in the recreation room, including the two warders who had defected to him. Hanson went back to the override panel and closed the two doors leading from the recreation room. Then he tuned the monitor to the maintenance airlock. Mashenko had come within range of the scanner and was standing opposite the inner door.

When Blanchard pushed the switch the inner door began to open slowly. He stood watching it, looking across the widening entrance at an angle. Too late he saw the recumbent space-suited bodies on the floor and realized their significance. Keegan fired his stun-ray through the half-open door and a figure crashed to the floor. Blanchard ran out quickly and cursed loudly. There was no mistaking the big Russian, even lying face down. He would be out for some time. Not only had they knocked out one of their own side, but now they had no earthly idea of what was happening and where to go. He thought quickly. "Come on, help me to carry him along here. We had better hole up in the workshop area for the time being." They dragged Mashenko by the heels through the doorway.

Hanson, horrified, watched as Blanchard and his convicts disappeared from the screen, dragging Mashenko with them. It looked as if their luck had finally deserted them.

Blanchard would not be familiar with the base and would be lost in the maze of corridors, each with its air-tight doors, linking the various working areas. A touch on the control panel focused the monitor on the workshop and showed him Blanchard and his men looking about them with an air of indecision. He would have to get to them somehow.

He switched the screen again to the recreation area. Here was something he had not bargained for. One of the space-suited figures had got hold of a laser and had already made a foot-long incision in one of the doors. Hurriedly he used the override panel to seal off another two doors on each side of the room. That ought to keep them occupied for a little.

As a precaution, in case Blanchard should take it into his head to leave the workshop, he sealed off one end of that as well.

Then, having operated the retaining catch on the chairman's door so that it would remain open, he peered cautiously into the corridor and sprinted along to the workshop. As he passed the unconscious guards at the airlock he picked up a stun-ray and gave them both another blast. He was not sure quite what effect that would have, but with any luck it should postpone their return to consciousness a little longer.

As he came through the door of the workshop Keegan swung round and raised his stun-ray. Blanchard called out, "For God's sake man, don't shoot." The convict looked genuinely disappointed as he lowered his weapon.

Hanson said, "Quickly, see if you can find some lasers—they use them here for cutting and welding. Try those lockers along the wall." He began going through the lockers himself, opening them one by one and rapidly scanning the shelves. One of the convicts shouted, "Here they are," and held up a small portable laser. They picked out three of them and tested them to make sure there was enough power in the batteries.

Hanson led them back to the chairman's office dragging the unconscious Mashenko with them. He would have a splitting headache when he came round. When they reached the office the monitor screen was still switched on and tuned to the recreation area. The man with the laser had almost finished cutting through the door and the other ten were grouped behind him.

By the time Hanson had finished explaining to the others what had been happening the rebels had succeeded in removing a rectangular panel from the door and all of them had rushed into the corridor. A moment later they came rushing out again and appeared to be arguing amongst themselves. Hanson wished there had been provision on the monitors for sound. After some hesitating and pointing at the other door they retreated to the corridor again.

Hanson drew a deep breath—it was now or never. In a straight fight they would be hopelessly outnumbered, even allowing for the lasers. There might be a chance if they could take them by surprise in the corridor. He went to the override panel and released the three doors on the other side of the recreation room. They would remain closed until the local switches were operated. They would have to trust to luck that one of the rebels would not come back and try them again. Before they left he returned the override panel to its secret position.

Speed was essential now and they bounded along the corridors which, like all the rest of the building except the gymnasium, were at moon gravity. The first of the three air-tight doors opened at a touch of the switch and they passed through into the next section of the corridor. Once inside it, Hanson turned to face them.

"There is one more door after this and then we come to the recreation room." He looked at Keegan. "You and I will go in first and the other two had better follow about fifteen yards behind. That way they will be outside the normal range of a stun-ray. Once we are inside the recreation room Keegan and I will go across quietly to the other door and you two will follow at the same distance. They should be almost through the second door by now and with any luck we should have them trapped in that section of the corridor. We'll take two stun-rays apiece and, as soon as we are in range, fire all four at once into them. The guns have enough spread to cover the whole width of the corridor.

"You Tony, and Deacon follow up with the lasers. If we get knocked out, all you have to do is to weave them from side to side of the corridor, but for God's sake, keep them clear of Keegan and me."

When they came to the second air-tight door Hanson put his ear against it and listened. There was no sound and he pressed the switch. It slid open with a slight hiss and they moved on towards the door of the recreation room itself, Hanson and Keegan in front, with the other two keeping a safe distance behind them. At the door Hanson paused again to listen and then, holding his breath, pushed the switch.

The door slid open and he relaxed—the room was empty. He beckoned the other two on and began to cross the room, Keegan trailing slightly behind. When he was almost at the doorway he motioned Keegan to stop and crept forward until he could see into the corridor. He withdrew his head quickly and whispered to Keegan, "They are about twenty-five yards along the corridor—out of range. We'll have to rush them. Don't fire until I shout and then fire both guns at once and keep the triggers pressed."

Keegan nodded and, at a signal from Hanson, they dashed into the corridor and ran towards the group at the other end. They had taken two strides when they were spotted and a shout went up. Hanson took one more enormous stride and shouted, "Now."

There was no sound. They staggered and fell to the floor as they were hit by the shock waves reflected back from the walls. Still dazed, they dragged themselves to their feet and surveyed the results. Hanson had not exaggerated the effect of four stun-rays fired simultaneously into the narrow corridor. Eleven bodies lay in a tangled heap and from somewhere there arose the sickening stench of burning flesh. They had not far to look for the cause. The man who had been cutting through the door had fallen on his laser which was still switched on. The beam had passed through his chest and through the neck of the man behind him. Hanson's gorge rose. He clamped his teeth together to contain it and carefully lifted the body until he could get at the laser and switch it off.

Deacon, who by now had come up with them, took one look at the still smouldering flesh and vomited all over it.

They dragged the bodies into the bar store where they locked them up and then made their way back to the chairman's quarters, laden with the captured stun-rays. Once there, Hanson tuned the monitor to his own office. There was no sign of Hughes, but he might be in one of the other rooms. Whoever had decided that the deputy chairman should be monitored had drawn the line at prying into his private quarters.

He took Deacon with him. Keegan might have been a more sensible choice, but he was trigger-happy and Hanson wanted Hughes for himself.

The outer door was locked and, motioning Deacon to stand clear, Hanson inserted his magnetic key. It slid open to reveal an empty waiting-room. The door to the office was wide open and he went in, the portable laser held in front of him with his hand on the switch. The room was empty, but he noticed that the converted stun-rays were missing. The other rooms were also empty. He picked up his space suit which was still lying where he had dropped it and together they went back to join the others.

"No luck?" Blanchard asked as they came in. Hanson shook his head. "We'll have to try the monitor, but I imagine he knows enough to keep out sight of the scanners." And so it proved. A thorough search of the base revealed no trace of him.

Hanson went over to the broadcast panel and switched on the public address system.

"Attention everybody, attention everybody. This is Roger Hanson, Deputy Chairman. Moonbase has been recaptured but there is one dangerous man still loose and he is armed with lethal weapons. Please stay where you are for the time being. You will be released as soon as we have rounded him up."

He paused, then began again, "You two men at the main airlock, put your guns inside the lock and then stand away from them. You are being watched on a monitor."

The erstwhile guards got to their feet, bewildered resignation showing on their faces. Blanchard and Deacon went to fetch them. When they arrived Hanson ordered, "Stun them. We can't afford to take any chances until we have Hughes in the bag." Deacon, who had so far not had an opportunity to use his stun-ray, complied with alacrity and kept his trigger pressed for a full thirty seconds on each.

Keegan, who had been passing the time studying the various control panels in the room, said suddenly, "There's a red light come on here."

Hanson went over. "That's the emergency hydrojet hangar—it must be Hughes." He turned to Blanchard. "Where did you leave the other machine?"

"Outside the main airlock."

"I'm going after him. He is probably making for the

reactors—he still has two men there and he has three lasers with him."

Hanson struggled into his space suit, secured his helmet and sprinted along the corridor.

Sealed in the hydrojet, Hughes feverishly scanned the control panel: Main Switch, Port Lateral, Starboard Lateral, Port Vertical, Starboard Vertical. He had not flown one of these machines before, but it seemed straightforward enough—a matter of applying the throttles gently until he had got the feel of it. First—Main Switch on, then open both lateral jets a touch. Gently the machine moved forward on its ramp, slid off it and hit the ground. He had forgotten the vertical jets.

Now he eased them open and the plane began to rise. So far, so good. He would follow the monorail to the reactor complex. He opened the vertical jets a bit more and the machine rose slowly to about thirty feet, then a touch to the lateral throttles and it began moving smoothly forward. The monorail terminal was on his right; that meant he had to open the port lateral wider. He did so and the machine spun like a top. Quickly he slammed the throttle shut and the starboard jet took over, rotating him more slowly in the opposite direction. After several attempts he got the machine under control and brought it over the first pylon of the monorail track.

As he turned to follow the line of pylons he saw the other hydrojet coming round the side of the dome. He swore under his breath—he had forgotten Blanchard's machine. There was still a chance—he had a slight lead and, what was more important, he had the laser guns. If he landed first he could use them before his pursuer could get out of his machine.

He slammed the lateral throttles wide open and the sudden acceleration thrust him back in his seat. When he had recovered his breath he looked back; the other machine had increased speed but was still some way behind him. He concentrated on the line of pylons which was curving away to the left in a wide sweep that demanded delicate adjustment of the jets. At six hundred miles an hour there was not much room for error.

Not trusting his feel for the throttles, he glanced down, closed the port throttle a fraction and looked up. Too much—he was circling away from the track. He looked down again and opened the throttle an even smaller fraction. When he looked up it was to see a wall of darkness rushing towards him. He had forgotten the terminator, the sharp dividing line between day and night on the moon. Too late he realized that he did not know where the light switches were. No time to look for them. He shut down the starboard throttle half way and the centrifugal force threw him across the tiny cabin. His knees collided with the control panel, shutting down the vertical jets entirely and almost closing the laterals.

Momentarily dazed by a blow in the head from the canopy, he struggled back to his seat and raised his eyes to see what seemed like a yellow wall in front of him.

Hanson eased back the throttles and brought the hydrojet round in a wide circle until it was hovering over the giant excavator. He watched the yellow scoop rise up and begin to tilt forward. Slowly the other machine toppled out and disappeared into the bucket, throwing up a slow-rising cloud of dust that gleamed near-white in the sunshine. The bucket tilted over and moved, incredibly slowly it seemed to Hanson, into the coils of the accelerator.

He pulled the lateral throttles wide open and the hydrojet hurtled towards the far end of the accelerator. By the time he got there Hughes's machine was a tiny white speck in the trail of rocks and dust setting off on their two months' journey to Alpha One.

FIVE

The sun was shining and champagne sparkled in the glasses. On the terrace, the scarlet and blue of the Matrician Order mingled with the latest creations of the London fashion houses which had never been so busy as during the past few weeks. It was without question the party of the year.

The occasion was the engagement of Roger Hanson, only son of Baroness Alicia Hanson, and Fiona, younger daughter of Baroness Mary Hamilton.

Leonora Fallon, *sans* husband, was in her element. Wearing a dress whose daring far outshone anything her dressmaker had previously achieved, she circulated among the assembled guests and, for once, the matriarchal frowns which usually followed her progress were nowhere in evidence. Not even the tiniest whisper of criticism was heard to mar the general air of happy festivity. The reason was not hard to discern. Next to Roger Hanson, her escort was the most sought-after man at the party. Mashenko, flushed with adulation and not a little champagne, beamed and bowed to kiss the extended hands as Leonora murmured name after distinguished name and matrician ladies of impeccable antecendents shamelessly claimed her acquaintance.

Her Excellency Hilda Kritzinger, Vice-President of Australasia, was chatting roguishly to Hanson senior who was having no difficulty in resisting her not very obvious charms. Not far away, Mme. Drasa Lubinka was discussing the new arrangements for security on the moon with the Commander of the Matrician Guard who was trying to maintain a deferential mien while seeking frantically to draw the attention of a passing servant to his empty glass.

Slightly apart from the rest of the throng, the Baroness Hanson, wearing a dress whose elegant simplicity was in marked contrast to the extravagant couture of her guests, was deep in conversation with Her Supreme Excellency Theodora Roosevelt Jackson, President of the Americas and Chairman of the World Praesidium. Her cheeks were flushed, though not with wine, and there was an unaccustomed sparkle in her eyes. She had just been informed that her nomination as Chairman of the Eurasian Senate and Chairman-elect of the Praesidium was secure. Next year she too would be a Supreme Excellency, a distinction which she valued almost as much as the barony bestowed on her great-great-grandmother.

Also a little apart from the other guests, the Baroness Mary Hamilton was seated in earnest conversation with Tony Blanchard, the story of whose dramatic rehabilitation was still the subject of amused gossip at matrician dinner-tables.

At Hanson's suggestion the Appeal Tribunal had assembled in a Gamma-class flat along with the victim of the crime and the two witnesses. On hearing the key words—"He's here. Come and get him" the men, who had been concealed in the bedroom, promptly rushed out and repeated their performance of a few weeks back.

The august matrons of the tribunal were not given to voyeurism and had tried to stop the proceedings when it became obvious what was going to happen, but they had reckoned without the effectiveness of hypnopaedia. By the time two warders had been summoned to drag the man off, the deed had been accomplished before their shocked eyes.

As he moved among the guests on the terrace, stopping to chat here and replenish a glass there, Roger Hanson was strangely out of tune with the evening. Try as he would, he could not shake off the thought that two people, without whom this party might not have taken place, were not there. He caught the eye of Wallis K Vanderbilt and threaded his way through the guests towards her.

"Congratulations, Roger. That was some job you did up there. What a pity that great little guy couldn't be here to enjoy it."

"I wanted to ask you about that. I understand you listened to the tape of his last message."

"Yes, but it wasn't very clear — there was a lot of static. The flight controller warned him that his trajectory was too flat and that he would bounce off the earth's atmosphere if he didn't correct it. Then there was a lot of interference and the only words we could make out were, 'must go' and something that sounded like 'fleet of stars'. Almost seemed as if it was deliberate."

Yes, Hanson thought, it was deliberate. Jimmy's life had reached its peak and he had chosen to go out in his own way, out into the vastness of Space which had captured his imagination so long ago.

Softly he repeated the words, "I must go where the fleet of stars is anchored and the young star captains glow."

The American's eyes widened. "Say, that must have been it. How did you know?"

"It's an old English poem about a dying patriot."

"Well I guess Jimmy was a patriot all right."

The inappropriate banality of the remark made Hanson wince and he sought for a suitably cutting reply, but at that moment Fiona came up. "I've been looking for you all over the place. It's a lovely party but there are too many people here — I want to get away from them for a little."

He took her arm and led her off into the garden. As they sauntered hand in hand under the canopy of trees Fiona looked up at him, her eyes wide with concern. "You seem a little sad. Is it those . . . who didn't come back?" He nodded, almost imperceptibly, and Fiona stopped, turning to face him. "I know you were fond of that girl — Sarah — but you must not blame yourself for what happened. She would not have wanted it that way. She died doing what she had always longed to do — and not many of us achieve that."

She stood on tiptoe and kissed him gently.